FROM HALLWAYS TO HIGHWAYS

FROM
HALLWAYS
TO
HIGHWAYS

High School Years
1974–1977

Gordon Mead Stewart

Campfire Stories

Cover illustration by Gordon Mead Stewart

It was a time of freedom and self-reliance that allowed for mischief and far-ranging expeditions.

Preface

What motivated me to write these accounts?

Over the past 15 years, memories of specific events in my childhood have tormented me constantly until I spend the weeks necessary to compose them on paper. During times when I have been writing about long-lost friends, we have often reconnected. My composition would then become part of our renewed correspondence. Because friends treasured them as a rare window into our past, these detailed memories appeared to be worth preserving.

Our way of life has changed drastically since this era. Hopefully, the spirit of these times is apparent in these "fact is stranger than fiction" exploits. Each story is self-contained, so feel free to time-travel among them.

Why are there so many different types of adventures?

During my high school years, I was battling scary juvenile rheumatoid arthritis (JRA). It is a rare and mysterious condition that occurs in only one in 50,000 people. It caused intense pain in every joint. Every day I was taking 18 aspirin to tolerate the pain and to avoid permanent damage. The next step would have been hazardous gold shots. My year in ninth grade was extremely harrowing during diagnosis and early symptoms.

Four times each day throughout my high school years, I was secretly swallowing a handful of aspirin, four or five at a time. It was a constant reminder to make the most of my time. No opportunity was over-looked. I was extremely fortunate to have so many excellent ones.

What process was used to write this book?

This flood of memories has been restricted to a trickle by my limitations. Each word has become precious. My youthful four-year JRA attack meant that problems might arise in later years, and that is what happened. After 2001, a vasculitis attack damaged my cerebellum, which weakened my motor control. It took years of treatment to battle it into remission. Being homebound ever since has been a blessing and a curse. It has freed my mind so that memories could surface, but typing a paragraph can take two hours.

When these relentless recollections come upon waking, I start scribbling notes on an iWatch face before the memories disappear. My waking hours are spent pounding out paragraphs on an iPad, rearranging puzzle pieces on a desktop, and much later marking up printout pages. Sometimes everything is then thrown out and restarted.

Deep Gratitude

Lifelong thanks to my parents for making me who I am with their love, intelligence, honesty, faith, and patience. My parents made their children's lives always their top priority. Dad has been an excellent role model who by his own recollections taught us to "live a life worth telling." Mom was always very loving and devoted to us. She first learned the full extent of these adventures while checking early drafts.

My lovely, smart, hard-working, complementary spirit from another continent, Jacqueline, is most deserving of gratitude for marrying, supporting, and putting up with me. The curiosity of our kids about these times has always been a big driver. Stories of mischief and more, kept from them as youngsters, can now be told.

A very special thanks to my friend and fellow adventurer since first grade, Matt Westbrook. A professional editor and highly respected poet, he used his expert eyes to shape my rough lumber into fine furniture.

And thanks to all the friends and relations, too many to mention, who have enriched my life and these stories. The unconditional love from so many has been a springboard into living fully.

Bowie Senior High School

What it was like going to one of the largest high schools in the United States in the 1970s? Bowie High was fortunate to be located in the center of Bowie, a planned community surrounded by an informal greenbelt. This gave us a unique advantage over the 21 other high schools in our Prince George's County (a Maryland suburb of Washington, DC). For example, Parkdale High School drew students from ever-changing boundaries of suburban sprawl, including parts of New Carrollton, Brentwood, Berwyn Heights, and Landover Hills. Elementary school friends might be split up among as many as three different high schools. Not in Bowie. Bowie's 14 elementary schools fed to three junior highs, which then fed into Bowie High.

Beginning High School

Imagine it's the summer of 1974. You just received your schedule to start 10th grade at Bowie High School at the end of summer. Among the 115 classrooms and 22 temporaries located on three levels, you have to locate your home room and the classrooms for each of your six periods on the tiny map that came with your schedule. The biggest question is this: where is your locker and whom do you share it with? Luckily, the sophomores start a day earlier than the 11th and 12th graders.

Lunch for 3,000 teenagers was a problem in an overcrowded school. The cafeteria and senior lounge could seat about 600—just right for three lunch shifts if the school had only 1,800 students. Some genius at the school board had planned to have a lunch shift between every period. From Student Government meetings, I learned that—thanks to the previous year's student protests—we instead would enjoy "open lunch." Open lunch was a one-hour break in the school day during which we were encouraged to eat lunch off campus, in the cafeteria, or in supervised classroom club meetings.

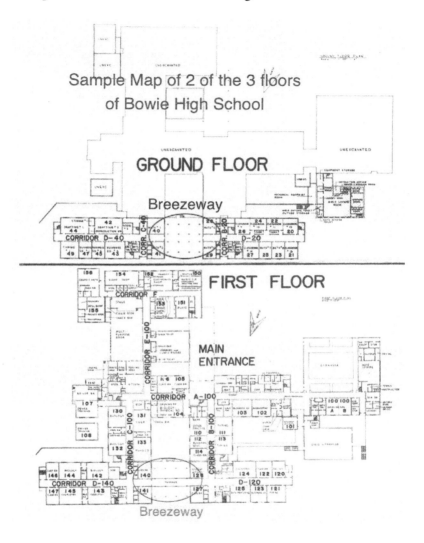

Sample Map of 2 of the 3 floors
of Bowie High School

GROUND FLOOR

Breezeway

FIRST FLOOR

MAIN
ENTRANCE

Breezeway

During open lunch, one part of the school, the "breezeway," hosted a microcosm of the three major school types. The middle floor was a glass corridor that looked out to the football field over the roofs of the temporaries and was fittingly where "jocks" congregated. Athletes in letterman jackets eyed cheerleaders, pom-pom girls, and fans. Under this bridge was an open area between the wings that was designated for smokers. These "freaks" weren't smoking only cigarettes, and they never wore coats, even in freezing temperatures.

On the top floor of the breezeway, offices flanked its corridors: guidance, career counseling, yearbook, etc. So, looking at a cross-section of the breezeway, there were: the freaks smoking outside on the ground floor, the jocks strutting and flirting on the main floor with a view of the fields, and the "nerds" on the top floor playing academic games and planning for careers. We were not very cliquey, however. Kids might major in one group and minor in another.

Getting There

Living in the K(enilworth) Section, we were way outside the walk-to-school radius, so we rode a bus. Our big, yellow school bus had only one bus stop a couple of blocks from my home. The bus had seating for 55, but our stop consisted of 70 riders. Back then it was still courteous for guys to give up their seats to girls. Therefore, our solution was to simply let all the girls on first so that they would get first choice of the insufficient seats.

But guys are still very competitive, and as our bus approached in the morning, a mass of jostling boys would crowd out into the street toward the moving bus. As soon as the bus stopped, the mass would part, leaving a passageway for the girls to enter the bus. Often, a little guy, Mike Meyers, would try to sneak on among the girls. He would be quickly lifted up and handed over our heads to the back of the mob. After the girls were on board, the guys would fight their way into the bus.

The guys standing in the center aisle tried to stay behind the driver's yellow line for the 10-minute ride to the school's front entrance. At the end of the school day, we just looked for our school bus number—printed on the side of each bus—and got in. The long line of 33 large buses filled the entry circle curve and went down the lane beside the school. Fortunately, the bus drivers tended to park along the same stretch of curb every day.

What Did We Wear?

Looking back through yearbooks, the class ahead of ours, 1976, was somewhat more "dressy"—dressy in that most girls wore dresses and guys wore collars. Starting in our class, the majority of the time, girls wore slacks. Wearing T-shirts and displaying company logos was not yet popular. There weren't any fluorescent-dyed, punk hairdos, piercings, or tattoos; no gangs or fights. The idea of uniforms in a public school was unfathomable. That was only for private schools. Bowie's only private school was St. Pius, grades 1 to 8, where students wore blazers and dark-green plaid skirts.

As you can see in the photo, no one had book bags or backpacks. We just carried our books. Our student population was about 8 percent black. There were no "magnet schools." Of our 980-student Class of 1977, about 85 percent attended college. As I learned to navigate the maze of Bowie High's classrooms and meet new people, little did I know the adventures that lay ahead.

Adjusting to the Light

Before we get deep into the high school years, I want to describe my job in the summers—lifeguarding. At age 15, it made sense to earn my lifeguarding qualifications, but this also required the ability to drive a car. So, in the summer of 1974 I rode my bike to the free three-week Driver's Ed course at the high school, and before the next summer, I had my driver's license.

It was a logical step up from the seasonal work of lawn mowing. Mom and Dad didn't want us to be holding down a job during the school year. Academics always came first.

At our Belair Swim and Racket pool club (BSR), our evening lifeguard lessons were held on top of a grassy slope near the diving board end of the pool. There used to be huge shade trees there that made it a cool oasis from the humid heat. We started with 14 students. Two dropped out after hearing of the testing and the price of the textbook.

We spent a lot of time, of course, learning how to save people. First it was swimming sidestroke while carrying a victim on our hip in a "cross-chest carry." Then repeatedly we lifted each other out of the pool safely. Lastly, we practiced CPR on "Resussa-Annie." Back then they were still recommending mouth-to-mouth resuscitation.

In addition to the physical, our training covered everything from tourniquets to heat stroke. It was very similar to the first aid that I'd covered extensively in Boy Scouts. Also, we were told that jumping into the pool to save a victim was a last resort if there was nothing to throw to them.

One on One

At the end of one class, we were introduced to "moonlight well wrestling." A guard would slip into each side of the diving well and try to pull the other back to their side. My opponent was the very voluptuous and intelligent Marian Keipert. I swam straight to the bottom of the 14'-deep well and waited while Marian's silhouetted form swam above. When I came up and put her in a cross-chest carry in a gentlemanly way, she seemed relieved.

Marian Keipert

The lengthy written test failed some students out of our class. More were dropped by the difficult physical tests. One of these tests required us to cross-chest carry a heavy, muscle-bound lifeguard on our hip the length of the whole pool, about 65 meters.

The Last Test

We had no idea what to expect. The test was held after closing time on a dark night. I was told to wait in the brightly lit men's restroom while it was prepared. Suddenly, a guy opened the restroom door yelling, "Help! Help!" and pointing toward the main pool. "Quick, someone needs help down in the well!" So, I ran on the concrete deck despite being told all these years to "Walk on the deck!" I could see a dark figure treading water.

The whole area was totally dark. Only the underwater lights in the pool were on. The victim in the water was the muscular guard we had saved during our other tests. We were used to finding him motionless; this time he was calling for help. The difference nudged me to resist jumping in.

"Don't Worry, I'll Help You." But How?

Everything was shrouded in darkness as my eyes fought to adjust. Then, I could barely see the outline of a life preserver far across the pool. That's never there! So, I peered into the darkness on my side. Another one was on a chair nearby. Holding one end of its rope, I threw it to the victim and pulled him to me.

At that point the testers came out of the darkness and congratulated me. Apparently, some people had frozen or just jumped in. As my eyes adjusted to the darkness, I couldn't believe all the possible saving objects they had placed just off the deck. There were metal poles, kick board floats, even a canoe! The real lesson was, "stop and think before panicking. Better options will become apparent." Only Marian and I passed the class.

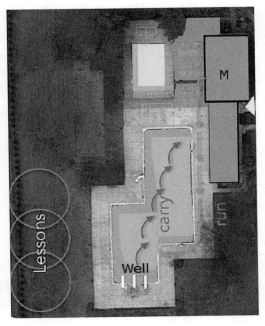

Getting Hired

A job was not a given once you had earned your "lifetime" lifeguard certification. "Belair at Bowie" was built for young families. This created a large number of kids near my age. Competition for available jobs meant employers could be highly selective. Earning lifeguard certification was no guarantee of a job—only a required qualification.

In the next week, Mr. (George) C interviewed me for a job for the next summer. He was in charge of all the lifeguards for three of Bowie's four pools. Belair Bath and Tennis (BBT) was the only Bowie pool he didn't control. This was my first-ever job interview.

Growing up at BSR and on its Barracuda swim team, we regarded BBT as a soft "country club" pool. They lost most of the intercity swim meets. We were Sparta compared to their Athens. They babied their lifeguards. Their guards were paid $2.30/hr., above minimum wage, but Mr. C paid us $1.75/hr., which was below. BBT also hired most of their guards from members and let them spend only half their time up in the guard chairs that were covered by umbrellas.

Sometime later, a letter notified me that I should report to Pointer Ridge pool club on a date a few days before next season. I had no idea where this pool was. At the time, the Pointer Ridge section was separated from us by a big swath of rolling, brush-covered land. Now it's a major part of "South Bowie." It was an afterthought, not part of "Belair at Bowie" proper. The Pointer Ridge pool was built around 1970 and was not Z-shaped like Belair's other three pools. Its shallow part was divided into a separate pool, so it wasn't possible for one lifeguard to watch the whole area.

Pointer Ridge's baby pool, 3' deep pool, and main pool

My first day was a cleanup and setup day. We pulled pool chairs out of the building and scrubbed their webbing clean. Most of this first year was a blur—just getting used to a regular job and a boss. An experienced guard was our pool manager. Their main power was in setting work schedules. Rookies like Marian and I had many 11 am-to-9 pm shifts.

One day she was working the check-in desk in her curvaceous bathing suit when the big boss, Mr. C, dropped by and said, "Somebody put a shirt on that girl up front. This is a family pool!" (Sorry, ladies, but these are a 16-year-old boy's memories.)

An Ocean City Road Trip

Toward the end of the first summer, I realized I was going to miss the beach that year. The lifeguarding work schedule had made it impossible to join my family's annual weeklong camping trip at the beach in Assateague State Park, even for a day. However, my next Saturday and Sunday were free, so maybe there was a chance to play in the waves.

At one of our toilet papering raids, John Cook said he also wanted to go. Being gamers, we naturally min-maxed our plans in order to make the most of our trip.

The traffic across the single span of the Chesapeake Bay Bridge could triple the three-hour travel time, and who wants to be stuck for hours in a sweltering car? Therefore, we left at sunrise.

"Sleep? Who Needs Sleep?"

We tried to catch up on our sleep on the gigantic endless sandy beach, but there was so much to see and do. Between body-surfing waves, we'd ask pretty teenage girls where the best dance places were.

The best place was somewhere on the bay side of narrow Ocean City, so we visited a few. Resort night spots with shifting clientele couldn't afford to turn anyone away with a cover charge, or card them for the legal drinking age of 18. Both of us were casual drinkers. Most everyone out was an "underage" teenager like John and me.

The place we settled on was entered by a pier that was docked by tall fishing boats. A fish much bigger than a man hung hoisted by its tail. John and I agreed on a rendezvous at closing time and were soon separated by the suntanned crowd. A raised deck with a bar led to another outside pier for a quiet escape from the dance floor.

Too soon, the 2 am closing time came, so we started the drive home in John's tiny two-cylinder Civic. Even taking turns driving, the weekend had caught up with us. I pulled over on the shoulder, and we were soon asleep. Our tiny car was rudely shaken awake by a passing tractor-trailer. In the mirror the sunrise gave me the time. Before us, the Bay Bridge gave the location.

Sent to My Home Pool

That summer my family's name came up in the five-year wait list to get into BBT. This made me eligible to guard at BSR, where I was next assigned.

Back in the BS(S)R

As my family's membership had moved over to the BBT pool club, my second summer of lifeguarding was back at my former home pool—BSR. Here I had finished my swim lessons, learned tennis, been on the swim team, visited by bike most summer days, and passed lifeguard certification.

Unlike my fellow guards, I knew most older kids at the pool. The little kids' names became familiar to me when I taught early-morning swim lessons. I could whistle and yell, "Walk, Tommy! If I have to tell you again, you're sitting five minutes under my chair." Teaching these BSR-sponsored lessons paid $3.00/hr. Parents asked me to teach private lessons, which paid much more.

Our whistle was our main tool for lifeguarding. It enabled us to "save lives" *preventively*. I never saw an emergency pool rescue. We applied many band-aids to boo-boos. There were some elderly heat exhaustion cases. The lanyard for my whistle was a black and yellow one that I wove at Boy Scout summer camp. You can get really good at twirling your whistle while sitting up in the chairs 45 minutes out of every hour.

To cool off while changing between the three chairs, it was nice to swim to the next one. This is where our special, always-comfortable guard suits helped. They would dry off quickly. The bold letters "GUARD" down each side made them especially attractive. Usually the pool was busy enough to warrant filling three guard chairs. A few days all four guard chairs were required, and during the Labor Day weekend a roaming fifth guard was needed as well.

Three chairs filled at BSR in 2017. The ragged tall tree was all that remained of our "shade trees on the hill."

Behind the Scenes

Despite appearances, pool lifeguarding is not all a glamour job. Whenever we were down from the guard chairs we were picking up trash, wiping down snack bar tables, or cleaning bathrooms.

One time I threw the hose on the restroom floor and went in the shower room to hook it up and turn on the water. Back in the restroom, I noticed the hose uncoiling and rising like a snake while shooting water knee-high. Too late I also saw that someone had just entered one of the stalls. Before I could react, the uncoiling hose passed under the stall door, soaking the occupant. I pulled on the hose and left the scene.

Because the next day's forecast was for continuous light rain, I looked forward to a day off. The pool was closed the next day, but we were told to wear a raincoat and old sneakers. We were all going to "HTH the decks." HTH is white granular chlorine that can eat holes in your sneakers, burn your skin, and irritate your eyes, but it sure does make the concrete decks white!

The pool manager hauled around a huge plastic construction bucket of HTH and scooped it out onto the deck. Using long-handled bristle brushes, we scrubbed it into every inch of the deck before rinsing it down the drains with buckets of pool water. The rain helped. So did breaking into song to make light of our miserable situation.

Before the Health Department came for their annual inspection, cleaning went into overdrive. Every closet was dumped of its contents and cleaned. We scraped up any gum with putty knives. Chewing gum was illegal around the pool, but some escaped detection. Our manager even had us weed distant sidewalks. I thought the Health Department should only inspect the snack bar, but they can close down a whole pool.

Relaxing Moments

As a prank, the Resussa-Annie mannequin was rigged up in the guard's locker room so that she swung down on the person who entered. The girls' screams were hilarious. Lifeguarding was ok, but with the availability of numerous summer internships in DC government offices, my two summers of lifeguarding were enough.

Guarding during pool parties paid a whopping $5 per hour. Since nobody went swimming, we took turns watching the pool from lounge chairs. Otherwise we mingled.

Performers

There was a group of little girls who used to practice their version of water ballet in the shallow end. Once they had their routine down, they'd call, "Hey, lifeguard. Watch this!"

Other performers often entertained the diving well guards. There we watched the amazing acrobatic and accurate diving by two guys my age, Eric and Brad. They were incredibly skilled divers, performing every type of dive beautifully, unlike me.

Following my father's example, I would do jack-knife dives off the low and high boards. It wasn't hard to go from those to one-and-a-half dives from each board, but I didn't enjoy flips or backward cut-aways. During flips you can't see the water to know when to untuck, and while doing a backwards cut-away your face might pass too close to the board. Besides, I liked landing way far out, close to the exiting ladder. Not Brad and Eric. They entered the water vertically without a splash.

That summer these two tried something sneaky in the restrooms. They climbed into the plumbing wall in order to peek into the women's showers. In the men's bathroom there was a wall that wasn't full height. After climbing down inside this wall, they could somehow shimmy into the plumbing wall. They were in this cramped location when a woman turned on a shower. The hot water pipe suddenly burned them. Shrieks came from inside the wall.

At the end of the summer, I was surprised when two little girls came up to my chair and gave me handmade cards. They weren't my only fans. At least twice in Bowie department stores like Sears and Peebles, older women would wink and say, "Almost didn't recognize you with your clothes on."

Everything Changed . . .

In 1992, I moved back to Bowie with my wife and two little kids. We bought a four-bedroom colonial fixer-upper that was five houses down from the BBT pool. It came with a BBT membership. It was fantastic for our kids. Our daughter, Lauriane, was even a lifeguard there for three years. It is truly a beautiful pool with a glimpse of the neighboring mansion. It was the first pool built in "Belair at Bowie."

1962 - 2002

Now lifeguards make a big deal about changing the chair guards. Two guards are never allowed to be up on the lifeguard stand at the same time. Back in our time, we would just climb up and tap the shoulder of the sitting guard and change places. Another way they are safer now is that each guard always carries a long rescue float.

A logo I designed for BBT's 40th anniversary

... Especially at BSR

It was shocking to return for a visit to BSR in 2017—40 years later. The first thing I noticed was that the entry circle flagpole was gone. We used to go outside the pool gates every day to the treeless entry area to raise and lower the flag. Now, huge trees were all around the circle and even in the circle. After passing through the new massive gate, I saw a new flagpole inside.

The snack bar was now covered, and the playground had new exercise structures, but the biggest change was that it seemed like our big trees on the hill had moved down to the flatland by the baby pool. I was very happy to see that they had kept and improved the high dive—unlike BBT, which changed theirs to an ultra-safe curly slide.

Gathered Together

County rules prevented Christian meetings on school grounds. However, some of my friends wanted to have a Bible study during open lunch, so they started meeting at a student's home nearby. We had many interesting discussions there and during our long walks back and forth. We felt like a tiny unwelcome group of secluded soul-searchers, but our devotion was about to blossom.

Sometime in 11th grade, I became aware of an outside-of-school ecumenical Christian group called "Young Life." They would meet at a different student's home every other Wednesday evening. I discovered that a friend in my homeroom, Adie Solomon (*second from right in photo*), was a major organizer.

How Would Everyone Know Where to Go?

In this pre-Internet age, a half sheet of mimeographed paper was the means of communication for Young Life. It was handwritten with the meeting place and time, as well as birthdays, celebrations, doodles, events, etc.

Adie had a woman in the school office clandestinely run off ditto copies. They were surreptitiously spread quickly throughout the school. Back then most people remembered that it is not polite to mention religion or politics—unlike now, when many wear chips on their shoulders, looking for either an argument or peer-pressure mob rule.

Our House

The first Young Life that I went to was in the High Bridge section. The carpet was filled with jeaned teenagers sitting cross-legged. It consisted of fun ice-breaking activities, a short skit, and lively singing. There was a short non-sermon. The enjoyable hour passed much too quickly.

Explaining this to my parents, I asked them if we could have a meeting at our house. When our turn came around, it was fortunately a fair-weather night. To make space in our 20 x 24-foot family room, we carried everything portable outside to our backyard basketball court. Chairs, sofa, end tables, and even the ping-pong table were moved, leaving plenty of space.

The family room and kitchen area quickly filled with teenagers. Some were even looking in through the open windows. The guitar player and youth leader had to stand on our long, raised hearth. We counted over 300 attendees. Most students

Young Life regulars eat lunch in front of the school. Our guitar player, Eric Sparrman, in the middle, is throwing a paper airplane.

specialized in only one activity; however, that night it was surprising to see a real mix of athletes, thespians, scholars, musicians, etc.

~

Young Life started in 1941 and has spread globally. Its website proclaims, "If teenagers didn't go to church, Young Life brought the church to them." Most of us were active in our individual churches, but it was nice to come together. Some Bowie kids went to a Young Life summer camp in Colorado. Much later, Adie and Eric, who happened to both be from my homeroom, became pastors of their churches.

A Is for Atkinson

In my first year (10th grade) at Bowie High School, I don't remember having anyone I knew from my neighborhood or elementary school in my homeroom or any of my classes. However, in French class and Homeroom I did recognize some classmates from Tasker Junior High.

It seemed strange to me that in high school, classrooms might have students from different grades. The course catalogues (for choosing next year's classes) deliberately obfuscated which classes were "advanced" versus regular. My Biology class in 10th grade was woefully slow-paced. By 11th grade they started removing words like "values" and "classic authors." A non-judgmental relativism was creeping in. Everything was equal. The school board wanted uniformity in students' abilities. Merit-based advancement was not allowed.

Mrs. Begor's Class

Fortunately, mathematics was still based on passing prerequisites. There were a few advanced Algebra sections taught by Mrs. Begor, who was a very good, experienced teacher. She was known for requiring our nightly homework to be written on carbon paper, which created a copy that we could hand in the next day. Having us sit in alphabetical order made it easier for her to go through the homework piles each night.

Mrs. Begor's alphabetical order placed "Atkinson, Douglas" in the very first seat, on the right side near the door. My seat was across the room, in front of the "end of the alphabet"

Mrs. Begor

column. Being of very quick wit, Doug was often the first to answer. He entertained us with his banter and questions for the teacher.

One day Mrs. Begor asked, "Oh Douglas, would you please stay after class?" Doug made an expression like, "Who, me?" and we all chuckled. While I was leaving class, she said that I might be interested too. That is how Doug and I became the first sophomores on the Math Team. We began riding to the Math Meets every two weeks with a group of about 12 and started rising through the B team. I'm not sure when, but sometime in the 11th grade, we began to earn time on the five-person A team. The A team composition fluctuated monthly depending on our recent performance.

Eleventh Grade Math with Mr. Lewis

Mr. Lewis, another experienced math teacher, also had our class seated alphabetically. This year Doug was again seated in the front of the class. I was back in the middle of my row. During slow moments I would pester Adie Solomon, who sat in front of me. It was very easy to make her blush or get her in trouble.

Mr. Lewis

During slow spells, I would draw in pencil on my desk. I might draw a small, detailed rendering of a horse. The next day I'd find that someone had drawn another horse. By Friday, our "canvas" would be full of horses. Over the weekend, the desk would be wiped clean. Next week the mystery artist and I might draw cabins, or cars, or trees. Years later, I discovered that my co-artist was Bob Feister, a longhaired rock musician.

One day, slow-talking Mr. Lewis was giving us an example of the commutative property of a certain mathematical operation. He slowly spoke his analogy, "Would it give us the same results if we opened the door and then threw Douglas out as it would if we threw Douglas out and THEN opened the door?"

Chemistry in Eleventh Grade

Our junior year, Doug and I were fortunate to end up in the same Chemistry class. Unfortunately, our teacher, Melodye Garner, was a first-year teacher fresh out of college. We never did hands-on experiments—just sat at our desks. "So, *this* is Chemistry," we thought.

Miss Garner

Miss Garner started teaching us at a college level, then back-tracked to fill in the prerequisite knowledge we lacked, leaving us all very confused. However, her first exam was based solely on her college-level teaching. Even worse, she left the room with the test answer key open on her desk.

When someone (sharpening their pencil) saw the test's answer key, it was quickly passed around the class. Doug and I, sitting near the back, refused to cheat. We tried our best before time was up. Days later, Miss Garner called both of us to the side. She said she knew we were smart in math, but didn't understand why we were the only two flunking her course. She asked us to grab our things and follow her into the lab prep room that was shared with the science class next door. Then, as she ushered us through the connecting door to the next class, she said that we'd probably do better in the class next door: Advanced Placement Chemistry!

Thrown into Merlin's Lab

As we made our way through the laboratory of this other class looking for the teacher, the number of experiments stunned us. The two of us, carrying our books, were like little hobbits entering Mordor. Bunsen burners were heating up solutions that were sparking, smoking, bubbling over with foam, or all three—like the mini volcano that one pair of students had made. The seniors saw us as a potential audience to practice on. One big, mustached senior showed us a snowball on his palm, then lit it on fire while still holding it. Two girls were adding drops to a beaker of clear liquid that instantly changed all the liquid to a solid color. Then they added drops of another color, which made it clear again.

We finally saw the AP Chemistry teacher, Dr. Mier, in his white lab coat, stopping by a different station. He was asking in his German accent, "Exactly which chemicals have you mixed together?" After the student rattled off the names of the chemicals, Dr. Mier exclaimed, "That's mustard gas! Quick—to the flame hood!" Everyone scattered, but nobody died.

Doug and I thought that this AP Chemistry was wonderful. We couldn't wait to do this kind of lab work every day. Apparently, that first day the class happened to be practicing for the next day's "Merlin Day"—a kind of chemistry magic show. We had quite a bit to catch up on, especially having never even taken "regular" chemistry. Looking back now, much of what was breakthrough news or just untested theories then shows up nowadays as just another fact in our kids' textbooks.

One example of this was the time that Dr. Mier showed us a movie, giving no introduction. You have to understand that Doug and I were fans of a new television show, *Monty Python's Flying Circus*. Dr. Mier's movie opened with a man standing in a funny way. Then, looking at the camera, he declared with a stilted British accent, "Today, we look for the elusive Quark." Both of us cracked up. This must be a humorous parody. No one would seriously name something "Quark," but everyone else was taking notes. This must be real!

In Chemistry, everyone had a lab partner. The problem was, the class had an odd number of students, and so Doug and I were partnered up with the intelligent "Jeannie" Miller in a group of three. Maybe this was because she also had labs to make up. Maybe she had volunteered to bring us up to speed.

Jeannie Miller

Although Jeannie was younger than us in years, she was a graduating senior. A troubled home life had matured her far beyond her years. Although she kept her life secret, sometimes a hint slipped out. Jeannie occasionally missed class. One time it seemed to be because she had to move in with someone. Maybe she didn't have a home, we thought. Where were her parents?

Like every other lab team, our team members took turns documenting the data of each experiment. Then the other partners would copy the data into their lab books. Doug always found it odd that whoever took the original notes received a grade of 9, while their partners got a 10. Somehow, we both earned an A in that class and took the AP Chem test.

Doug made sure he earned an A in every class. Whenever a teacher's test grading methods created ambiguities, he let them know. He kept them on their toes.

The Downpour

Here's another anecdote about that Chemistry classroom. There was a huge sunflower-sized showerhead hooked up to an emergency chain. Rumor had it that the number of gallons dumped by pulling the chain could fit in one standard tall wastebasket (4' high, 2' in diameter). Chuck Ulrich, another of our friends, had access to the lab after school and, smiling, showed the showerhead to a few of us.

Chuck Ulrich

Before we knew it, "Monkeyman" Chuck had put the tall wastebasket underneath and pulled the shower chain. We watched with trepidation as the water rose closer to the top. When it finally stopped, we knew we were in big trouble. Where could we put all that water? In answer Chuck said, "That's easy! Just throw it out the window."

"But the window louvers have small openings," we protested. Laughing, Chuck replied, "Not the fireman's window!" He pulled that window's red lever and swung it open. Somehow, we "nerds" were strong enough to dump the water out. It landed on the sidewalk two floors below. Unfortunately, at that time, the soccer team was jogging by on the way to practice. Doug, who played on the team, told us how it made the coach livid.

The World's Sport Comes to Bowie

Somehow Bowie experienced an instantaneous soccer boom in 1974. It's hard to believe now, but before that year, most of our little world had never even heard the word "soccer" or seen one of those panda-colored, geodesically stitched balls.

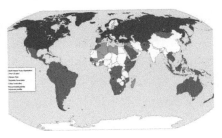

A major event that might have helped trigger this boom was the 1974 World Cup in Berlin. Maybe people saw snippets of it on *The Wide World of Sports*, a Saturday afternoon TV show. Maybe it was because everyone felt freer since the end of the military draft and the coming end of the Vietnam War.

America was still in a very dangerous "Cold" War against the Soviet Union. This World Cup was held in West Berlin, an embarrassing thorn of freedom in the Soviet bear's face. A few days after our Fourth of July that year, West Germany, our frontline ally, won the World Cup. It was a symbolic victory for democracy and even made our parochial news.

Soccer was considered an expensive private-school sport like field hockey or lacrosse. Fortunately, I had a big head start in soccer. During my first year at Queen Anne, a small private school, the bespectacled British Mr. Bowring had coached our JV team. Besides outlining the rules and strategies, his blackboard talks showed us how to "make space" (in American, "get open") and form "W" shapes with three men spread out in front of two. He would often chide defenders in his very proper English accent, "When in doubt, kick out!"

The next year, in eighth grade, Will Hart and I were unexpectedly promoted to the varsity team. It wasn't due to my dexterity, although I was one of the few who could kick with either foot. Endurance wasn't my strength either, but, like my cousins, I was a fast sprinter. The main reasons we were both promoted to the varsity team was our awareness and our lack of fear when challenging opponents for the ball.

Playing soccer in the BSA

In the fall of 1974, my whole family (except three-year-old Heather) suddenly became deeply involved with five different newly formed Bowie Soccer Association (BSA) teams.

Five Soccer Teams that Autumn

We three brothers were on three different soccer teams due to our different ages. Also, my 13-year-old brother, Jeff, volunteered to help coach our little brother Colin's team. Then 7-year-old Colin was chosen for a select travel team, but Jeff kept helping with Colin's previous coach, John Sullivan. He said Jeff was really the main coach each time he picked him up. As if four teams weren't enough, our parents played on a fifth team.

Their team was in a "Rainbow League" that was only for those over 35. It was a real switch to see the kids on the sidelines cheering their parents on the field. One day there was a hotshot former European pro-soccer player on the other team. We all cheered when Mom adroitly stole the ball from him.

My team was for 15- to 17-year-olds. With all the Kenilworth kids on my team, it was clear that the BSA had created teams based on neighborhoods. The fields we played on weren't the hard-as-concrete elementary school fields, but the thick grass-covered fields near Allen Pond. However, by season's end, there was often a huge puddle on one side of the field. At the beginning of some very cold-weather games, players would be hesitant to dive in after a floating ball, but soon everyone became very muddy.

During this first year our coach was Mr. Vittorio, who used to play on a professional Italian team. He named our team "Juventas" which means "youth" in Italian. Most of our players kicked the ball with their toe like in elementary school kickball. He urged everyone to use the inner instep of our cleats to gain more control. Also, he explained that when a pass came from your right, it's best to field it with your left foot.

After going to two practices a week and a game on Saturday, I realized it was too much for my joints. The previous year had been a very trying one of visiting doctors to diagnose my main symptom, painful and hot inflammation in all my joints. It was finally diagnosed as JRA, juvenile rheumatoid arthritis, which is very rare. It seemed to be caused by an agent that only affects those predisposed to it. Dr. Sills, the Johns Hopkins doctor who finally diagnosed it, mentioned some curious case where it affected many sailors aboard a ship.

JRA usually lasts three to five years. Permanent damage might be minimized with medication. Throughout high school I took 18 aspirin a day, often five at a time, and escaped with only slight damage to my back. Fortunately, the pain in my every joint was reduced enough that I was able to avoid more severe treatment like gold injections. Mr. Vittorio was sympathetic and let me miss some practices. After going full-tilt each Saturday, I faced a painful week before recovering just in time for the next game.

Playing Equipment

Some of our registration fee paid for the great referees. The rest was for our very heavy two-sided BSA jerseys. One side was dark red, while the other was blue. Usually, the schedule correctly indicated which team wore which color. If both teams arrived in the same color, it was easy for one team to switch by turning their shirts inside out.

We wore a variety of shorts and socks. Longhaired Bobby Porsche wore a headband that made him look like an Indian. I wore my favorite blue-and-yellow-striped white Queen Anne socks over my old shin pads. Wearing them I felt like a tank that could run through walls.

My parents were always surprised at how their polite son turned into an aggressive animal on the field. I was in an environment with different rules. It is like the shy kid who, once on stage, belts out a song. Aggressiveness made all the difference in our games. Accurate passes were rare, so there were many "50/50 balls." Whoever was boldest won the ball.

Formation

Queen Anne and BSA teams used the "2-3-5 formation," which is outdated now. Simply put, the two big guys who could kick the farthest played the two defensive "fullback" spots closest to our goal. The five front line players were, therefore, usually smaller. At Queen Anne, I played left wing on the front line because, as an eighth grader, I was small compared to the towering 11th and 12th graders.

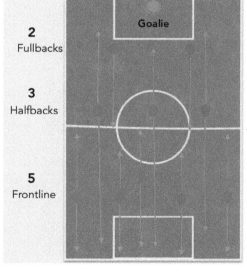

Because I could kick left footed, I played left halfback during my BSA years. Mr. Vittorio developed a great secret strategy based on the fact that some of the other key players and I didn't have the stamina to play the demanding position of halfback for the whole game. During the first quarter, our team's strategy was simply to tire the other team out by having them chase the ball that our team kicked back and forth across the field.

Even if the other team scored in the beginning, we still had the inner confidence that we could win. Games were low scoring, and each goal was dear. One time I was running at full speed toward the left side of the goal to redirect a crossing shot. The next seconds seemed to happen in slow motion.

The ball was coming from my right, so I kicked it with my left foot. This caused me to spin toward the goalie, who deflected my shot out toward my charging teammate. Not having time to react, he sent the ball back my way. Stumbling back toward the post, I realized that the ball was going to barely miss the goal. As it passed behind my back, I tapped it in with my right elbow just before hitting the pole with my spine.

Unaware of the results, I collapsed on the ground. When I recovered, I learned we had scored! Either the ref didn't see my elbow, or he rewarded my effort and self-sacrifice. We advanced to the final and won the first BSA "City Championship."

Skipping a Year

To provide more time to tackle my class work and get good grades for college, I decided not to play BSA soccer in 11th grade. However, during my third year of college I looked back on my high school grades to help decide if I should play on the Architecture School's intramural soccer team. It turns out that my best grades were during the two fall semesters when I was playing competitive soccer.

Returning to Juventas

In the fall of my senior year, Mr. Vittorio was no longer coaching, so Dad stepped in as our coach. My brother Jeff was now old enough to join the team, so our family's soccer schedule was much easier. Our team included Mike Marion, whom I could telepathically pass to without looking; tall Mike Thompson, who could send his two-handed throw-ins right in front of the goal; and young Tommy O'Connor, who made the sideline along his wing position like a wall. He fielded every ball kicked his way.

Mike Marion   *Mike Thompson*   *Tommy O'Connor*

To win the city championship game, we had to score on the opponent's amazing goalie, Brian McLean. He hadn't been scored on all season. His team, Mr. Wannemaker's, had only been scored on once, and it had been during a game that Brian had missed.

On game day, knowing that we had to score early, I was ready to race across the centerline for our opening kickoff pass. As I started to sprint when the whistle blew, the opposing wing, Neil Manheimer, cleated my foot and pushed me over. I saw his smirk before he ran to the other end of the field. In class, he and Wannemaker's son would always whisper, point at people, and giggle.

The only way to get back at him was to win. One of our defense kicks went over everyone onto their side of the field, so I sprinted after it. Only their goalie was between me and the goal. As I was approaching the point where the ball would hit the ground, I saw their goalie unexpectedly running towards me. He was way outside his box. I tried to lower myself and go under him. Somehow he miraculously grabbed the ball as we collided. I was given a red card and thrown out of the game.

The league commissioner, Mr. Vittorio, who had witnessed our collision, much later overturned this call, so I was allowed to return in the second half. We managed to score twice on Wannemaker's team, more goals than they'd allowed all season! It may have helped that their goalie was now batting away our shots rather than catching them. Our Juventas team managed to win the city championship for the second time!

Felled by Microbes

Spring soccer was much more lax, being more like pickup games. There were no practices, only Saturday games. If one team didn't have enough players, some players switched sides by turning their shirts inside out. We might even balance the teams if one was dominant. Our team water bottles were typically old one-gallon plastic milk jugs filled with water that had been chilled in someone's freezer before the game. We would hold one overhead by the handle and drink without touching our lips to the jug.

After the season, I started feeling incredibly tired. When it turned into a sore throat and feeling feverish, a doctor's visit diagnosed it as mononucleosis. Eventually, we noticed that half our soccer team had come down with mono. If this was the "kissing disease," we couldn't have all dated the same girl. Then someone remembered that a woman watching the game had let her young son, who was feeling bad, drink directly from a jug. This act left me unable to attend our Senior Prom, but I recovered enough for the last weeks of class.

Don't Look Down

Even though she was a year younger, Janice Pritchard invited me to a meeting of a just-forming "high-adventure" Explorer post. It was based in New Carrollton, a short drive away. This proved to be the best gift this 15-year-old boy scout could receive. There was a large Explorer post in Bowie, but it focused on boating and sailing and required a major time commitment. It seemed that Explorers would be similar to Boy Scouts, but for teenagers and with girls.

We were dropped off on a weeknight at a brick rambler. Lanky Mr. True and petite Mrs. True warmly welcomed us. Inside we joined about a half-dozen others our age sitting cross-legged on the carpet. Leaning forward in his chair, Mr. True started out by discussing an upcoming rock-climbing day. They were finalizing the logistics. The trip was that weekend, and everyone was going—including me!

This was so much more relaxed and informal than scouting. There were no uniforms, ceremonies, or handbooks. It felt too unreal to have a post number. Janice had told me that, for the first months, I would be there on a conditional basis. Mr. True would decide if I got along well with the group. Also, schoolwork came first. This was much better than my previous Scout troop, which had a couple of screwballs who caused problems and then were promoted to leaders and created even more chaos.

Throwing Yourself Off a Cliff

Our destination was the ragged, well-worn cliffs on the Maryland side of the Potomac downstream from Great Falls. We arrived bright and early to reserve a good spot with a 40- to 50-foot drop in Carderock

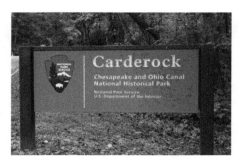

Park. After walking a couple of minutes from parking, you can top-rope down. The water is not far, but it's hidden by the dense foliage.

Mr. True happened upon the best guide for us. Our teacher was Chris, a weathered, stout, South American mountaineering expert. He had grown up climbing the Andes mountains in his backyard. He knew what to watch out for. He had been on climbs lasting for many days in which the climbers had slept in hammocks on a cliff face. Sometimes not everyone returned.

We each took a 12-foot-long strap of white nylon webbing. Mimicking Chris, we tied a couple of special knots a few inches away from our strap's center. After that it was pretty easy to run the ends though your legs, one around each leg, through each knot, and around your waist. The ends were smoothly tied together with another type of knot. Nothing went over your shoulders.

A D-shaped locking carabiner (*right*) went around all straps in front of your groin. It would be the attachment point for the oval rappelling carabiner with its brake bar. The harness and D ring were tested by being tugged

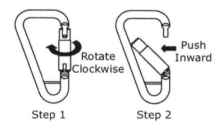

upward by Chris. The harnesses were surprisingly comfortable after adjusting them over your jeans.

One of the most important lessons was how to loop the climbing rope over the "brake bar" of the oval carabiner (*right*). It opens and locks in only one direction. People had plummeted to their deaths by having a wrongly strung brake bar pop open.

Over the edge of the cliff was a double strand of climbing rope firmly anchored to the base of some trees a dozen feet back from the edge. At the cliff's sharp corner, the rope was protected from damage by a carpeted car floor mat. Even though they were very expensive, a climbing rope must be discarded if ever left alone with a dog, according to Chris.

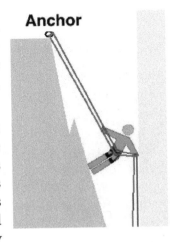

Anchor

When it was your turn to rappel, you straddled the rope with your back to the cliff. After correctly looping both strands through your oval carabiner and over its brake bar, you grasped the front strands with your right hand. Likewise, you pulled up the rope behind you with your left. By pulling your left hand to your side and forward, the increased friction would slow the passage of the rope across your palms.

Stepping into the Void

By far, the most difficult part is walking off the cliff backwards. At the edge you must lean back from a vertical position into a horizontal. Only by staying horizontal can you fend off the cliff face with your feet while controlling your descent. Your life could end if you falter.

At first, my descent was controlled. It was a lot to think about while playing the line out through my gloved hands. About halfway down I started losing control. Not able to pull my left hand forward, I just kept gripping tighter as I sped downward. It hurt when the back of my thighs hit the ground. Embarrassed, I jumped up before anyone saw. The glove surfaces had become too hot to touch.

The way back up was long and winding. Much of it was clambering over rocks. A pile of discarded sweaters and sweatshirts began to grow up top. My work gloves joined the pile. Bare-handed it was easier to work the rope. Everyone was pretty good after rappelling a couple of times. There's nothing like the exhilaration of flying down a cliff using only slight hand motions and light bounding jumps. Next was cliff climbing.

Mutually Trusting Our Lives

Climbing the cliffs required someone to catch you when you inevitably fell. Chris demonstrated to us on a much smaller cliff. Standing at the top, he dropped a line. It was attached to me. I wasn't sure about being the guinea pig, but Chris was able to catch my falls even though he was merely feeding the rope around his back.

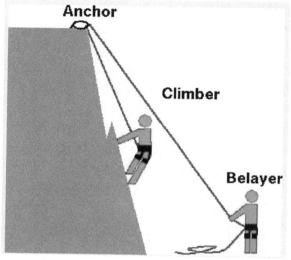

Now we "belayed" each other. At a nearby full-height cliff, another line was similarly anchored up top. One end would be tied to the climber while the person belaying would hold the other rope around their back. They would take up the slack as the climber progressed up the cliff. Incredibly, the littlest girl could catch the biggest guy due to the friction in the system.

Our system was that after rappelling down the other cliff, you would walk over to belay a climber. When they tied on the rope, they would call, "Belay." Once you had pulled up the slack and were ready to "catch" them, you replied, "Belay on." As soon as they were ready to start up, they'd yell, "Climbing" and wait for your "Climbing on." After belaying someone to the top, it was your turn to climb.

We didn't have the chalk bags or special climbing shoes of the other more experienced climbers. Like most of our group, I had ankle-high, treaded hiking boots. Of course, nobody wore helmets.

The Man in Black

There was a pathway along the base of the cliffs. Occasionally people passed by who were dressed like us. However, at one point a gentleman in suit and tie showed up. He curiously asked about what we were doing and how our gear worked. His shiny dress shoes made me wonder if there was a church around the bend. Then he went on his way.

I climbed most of the way up, then stopped for a rest because above, it became more difficult to find holds. This position had fairly good toe and finger holds. To my left was a gorgeous view. Over the treetops I could see our rappelling cliff. Up top, the formally dressed gentleman was talking to an obviously flustered Mr. True.

What happened next almost made me lose my grip. The gentleman quickly bent forward and ran head-first off the cliff. I waited for the thud. Somehow, he had stopped his fall before the bottom, turned to vertical, and walked away.

A Carderock cliff climb by others

Later we discovered that he was an Army Ranger. They trained to rapidly descend unknown cliffs face-first. They wouldn't know how far the drop would be and had to hold their rope one-handed because the other hand needed to be firing a weapon. At the bottom they had to quickly run for cover.

Just the Beginning

This was an amazing and rare opportunity with a wonderful group of people. It was so well run and organized. I still have never talked to anyone from another Explorer post, nor heard of another one, with a "high adventure" theme. Our many adventures were exciting and fun.

This first experience was in the fall of 1974. I only missed a couple of outings during the next three years before graduating from high school. Janice missed none, and being a year younger than me, she enjoyed another year before graduating and going off to college.

We went a few more times to Carderock for its other cliffs. Later we climbed the much higher cliffs at "Big Devil's Stairs" somewhere in West Virginia. The hike was difficult because of all the loose rock.

The business card that Chris gave to Mr. True. Online you can find Chris's accomplishments under many different listings. His "business" list was the same as our Explorer post's!

Twisted ankles were a constant concern. Because the cliffs were made of easily fragmented rock, there were a couple of close calls.

But that's for a future telling.

Underworld

Our next month's outing after rock climbing was a cave exploring day trip. During the Explorer post meeting, these simple caving rules were emphasized: stay together, always have three sources of light, and wear footwear that you don't care about. After caving, your shoes become so dirty and smelly that they are only useful for future cavern crawls. I used an old pair of lawn-mowing sneakers.

Our style of carbide lamp

The temperature deep underground is a constant 54 degrees, so we dressed accordingly. We didn't wear knee and elbow pads; our thick clothing was enough protection. Like some others, I had a jumpsuit over my clothes to prevent snags. It was the kind that car mechanics wear.

Headgear

Trying to fit into a sample helmet demonstrated my perennial hat problem, my large head. Luckily Dad was able to bring a big one home from NASA. It was made of smooth brown fiberglass. Importantly, it had a metal bracket in front for mounting a lamp.

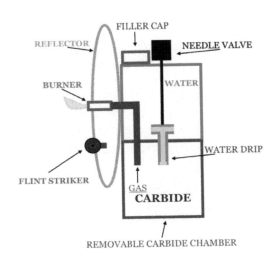

41

We used typical carbide gas miners' lamps. They have a small gas flame jetting from the middle of a broad round reflector plate. This casts a broader, more diffuse beam than battery-powered lights and weighs less. If someone crawled up too close behind, you felt the heat. Janice even embroidered a colorful design on the back pocket of her jeans, depicting a light with the words, "Watch That Light!"

The caves that we explored over the years didn't have the marked trails, electric lights, or handrails of tourist caves. Nor were they like the fictional hole in the cliff with a flat dirt floor. In fact, most of these "local" caves were simply a hidden hole in the middle of a rural field. It was surprising that first caving morning when we stopped in the middle of nowhere. Mr. True had to figure out which bush to look under. After squeezing in, we began our long descent.

As you continue downward, you are mostly busy playing something of a follow-the-leader trying to figure out the best way under, through, over, or around the various obstacles. The passageways zig, zag, constrict, and expand in a random fashion. After many hours into our first cave, we reached a large room. We found seats on large, flat boulders facing the entry.

While catching our breath, the reality of our situation increasingly filled us with wonder. First, we learned that over our heads there was over a mile of earth. Above the room's entry was a precariously supported cube of rock the size of a two-car garage. You could see from the sides that it had broken from the ceiling and was being balanced at a couple of corners.

To truly feel the "absolutes," we all turned off our lights and sat still. There was absolutely no light, no breeze, and no sound. On our way out, all previous landmarks were unrecognizable. Back on the surface you feel a renewed appreciation for what you'd been taking for granted.

A Few Local Caving Experiences

The local caves like Crabtree in far Western Maryland were fairly easy. Although I don't remember the names of the later, more challenging day-trip caves, I can't forget a few situations. They all happened deep underground, hours from the surface.

In one cave there was a 50-foot-long narrow crawlway. The ceiling was too low to fit inside with your helmet on; you had to slide it along in front of you. There was a trickle of water running down the middle. You had to slither, not army-crawl. I tried that and got my elbows stuck by my sides.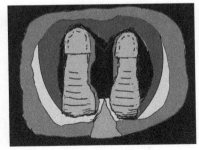
The person behind me had to pull my foot in order for me to free my arms.

At the halfway point was a spot that was tall enough to allow us to get up into a crawling position. You had to be careful, though, as you came to the end of the crawlway. It ended at the face of a small underground cliff. It was only about an eight-foot drop, but it took some careful contortions to extract yourself while grabbing for handholds.

~

The second incident happened after a few of us had come back to the larger room. Sitting down, we wiped enough mud off our faces to eat granola bars and take a drink. All of sudden, Beth yelled, "Kathy! Your hair's on fire!" We got her helmet off and patted out the fire. Apparently, the lamp's carbide liquid had leaked and run around the rim of her helmet. There wasn't any significant damage.

~

The third occasion was in a different cave. It was nightmarishly scary. We had been crawling and climbing in our usual single-file manner. I was last in line. Usually each obstacle didn't take long to figure out how to overcome, but because we were all of different sizes and abilities, it often required a unique squirm and maneuver.

However, this seemingly endless challenge was different. As the cave walls got closer and closer, the floor and ceiling disappeared. We were supporting ourselves on the nubs of two opposing cliffs, and the passage was too narrow to turn our helmeted heads. Pushing with our backs on one cliff helped us press our hands and feet against the opposing one and inch forward.

A large drop of water from somewhere far above fell past my outstretched hand and disappeared into the depths below, forcing me to wonder how far I would fall if I slipped. Would I eventually get lodged between the opposing walls? As I pressed forward, the occasional pounding of more drops on my helmet urged me to hurry.

About ten feet ahead, the passage became blocked. It was huge Clifford Fox. "I think I'm stuck," he said in a soft voice. "It's getting too narrow to go forward." After a few minutes of searching in the dim light, he started to panic and said that he had to go all the way back, but we were unable to turn our heads. It could have been fatal.

We tried to call for the others, but they couldn't hear us. After a long discussion, we figured out that the small girls before us had climbed downward and then continued. I guided him back a few feet. Going downward about a body length bought him enough width. We managed to get out, but it seemed to take us forever.

Caving Heaven

During the summer of 1976, we spent a week at the ultimate caving location, Mammoth Cave. With 400 miles of cave explored and documented to date, it is the largest natural cavern in the world—longer than the next two longest caves combined, according to park info. Back when we went, two of our group spent days with a team that was discovering and mapping sections never seen before.

The trip to western Kentucky didn't seem that long, probably because I was in a car full of other teenagers. Nowadays, the drive from the DC area is estimated at nine hours. It must have taken us more than 11 hours, considering what happened to the True's vehicle.

Somewhere near Kentucky, our two-lane road started a steep descent down through extremely sharp hairpin curves. As our car slowly followed the True's station wagon around each bend, we would shout and wave our arms out the windows.

We became quiet when we heard a rattling sound from their car, which grew louder at each turn. It turned out that the lugs were shearing off and rolling around in the hubcap. The left rear wheel was only being held on by two remaining lugs. The car was towed back up to the garage that had just patched the tire. By over-tightening the lug nuts, they had almost caused a disaster.

When we arrived at our destination, an old abandoned farmhouse, we slept soundly in our sleeping bags on the floor. It turned out to be a camp spot for serious cavers. One evening we were sitting dangling our legs off the edge of the front porch when a dusty figure approached. Under the brim of his helmet there were deep, dark recesses where his eyes should have been. Not breaking his stride over the hardpacked soil, he magically turned and walked up the steps.

That evening while his friends swapped stories, we learned of this blind caver's many feats. He could corkscrew out of a tiny hole in an underground cliff, then reach up around an overhang to quickly find a handhold to support his weight. His light was only for his friends to track him. When it went out, it was hard to find him due to the cave echoes.

Bedtime Stories of the Most Infamous Cave Explorer

In 1925, a veteran cave explorer named Floyd Collins was searching for another entrance to the Mammoth Cave system. As usual, he was exploring by himself and armed only with a lantern. Far from the entrance, his foot became trapped. He struggled in the darkness, but moving only brought down more debris. Twenty-five hours later, he was found still alive.

 During one of the early attempts to save Floyd, a young, intrepid reporter was one of the few brave enough to reach him with sustenance. Soon newspapers across the country were reporting daily on what became the first truly national news coverage. After many attempts to rescue him, Floyd died, having been trapped for 14 days. When they finally dug down to the rock that had fallen on his foot, it was lifted easily.

Later, a subsequent owner displayed the body of Floyd Collins in a glass-topped coffin as an attraction in their Crystal Cave. A rival cave owner stole the body and threw it in the Green River. It was recovered and put back on display, minus the damaged leg. The detailed story can be read online by searching "the 1925 cave rescue that captivated the nation."

Back to Our Caving Week

The two most adventurous of our group that had been with the team finding and mapping unknown portions of the cave complex would relate their exploits. One time they helped remove enough of a pile of fallen rubble to gain access to a never-before-seen passageway. Another time they had to quickly climb out of a chamber. Their lamplights were growing dim and breathing was difficult. It was a "dead-air room."

By far the most breathtaking highlight of our week was a special tour. Not many had been given access to this room because of its extremely delicate formations. We had to leave our helmets with their lamps extinguished in a previous space and rely on our guide's flashlight.

The low ceiling required a crouched, crawling position, but the room was wide. Growing out of the walls and part of the floor were delicate, curling, plant-like formations. They defied gravity like frozen seabed flora. You could see why they were once believed to be the thoughts of the devil. They may have been "helictite bushes." How they form is still a mystery. Photos cannot do them justice.

Helictites in Spain

Our Last Day's Trek Back to the Farmhouse

The mass of limestone that we had been under all day was off to our left. A keyhole opening in the wall behind some brush caught my attention. A few of us were able to squirm inside. The low rays of the sun revealed that the chamber opened out for a dozen feet before coming together in a narrow crack.

This little cavelet was teeming with life! In other caves we only had clumps of dark-colored bats hanging from the ceiling. We had to be careful because disrupting their hibernation cycle could kill them. Here there were many colorless crickets and spiders not far from the entrance. Along the floor was a shallow trough of crystal-clear water.

Inside were goldfish-like fish that were totally transparent. You could see each one's organs and beating heart!

We couldn't stay long; we had to run to catch up with everyone else on the trail. As we headed back, we didn't know if we'd return, but we all knew this: cave exploring can't be put into words. It's truly an indescribable experience.

Corbin Cabin

Our Explorer post wisely went dormant for the holiday season, but not for the whole winter. During February's long Washington birthday weekend, we'd be "pioneering" in a log cabin. My expectations foresaw a cooped-up endurance test. A "log cabin in the winter" sounded like a brown-and-white-striped confinement.

Mr. True, as a member of the Potomac Appalachian Trail Club (PATC), had been able to reserve a primitive PATC cabin during this coldest month of the year. It was a four-mile hike from the road. A creek and an outhouse would be our outdoor plumbing.

At the Trailhead

In order to "be prepared," I overpacked. Not trusting in the cabin's cookware, I brought my mess kit. Wrongly expecting down time, I also included a big Foxfire book of Appalachian folklore. My "modern" blue backpack was bulging once we divided up the provisions. My inexpensive green sleeping bag hung underneath.

The easy-to-follow trail sloped slightly uphill. The heavy gray sky cast no shadows onto the carpet of brown leaves. We eventually reached the noisy Hughes stream that had been running off to our left. After fording it by rock hopping, the trail led us further upward.

This gradual pilgrimage was transformative. Our many steps through nature had removed civilization's dust from our soles. Clear creek water now filled our canteens and quenched our thirst. Fresh mountain air refreshed our hatless heads and open coats.

The trail leveled and started downward. The uniform tapestry of vertical gray trees pulled back, revealing a small clearing around a cozy cabin. A dark metal roof sloped down over its welcoming low porch. A massive grey stone chimney buttressed its side. Behind and below this mini monotone masterpiece, a brook babbled softly.

Breathing Life into the Sleepy Abode

The windows were all shuttered with unadorned slabs of wood. They could only be opened from the inside. While Mr. True was on the

porch unlocking the wide front door, I noticed a narrower door to the right, labeled "Bunk House." This room had no internal access to the rest of the cabin. In the heat of summer, it was a refuge from the hot chimneys on the other side. It was left locked.

Soon all windows and shutters were opened. Supplies were organized, sleeping bags unrolled, lanterns prepared, and water ported up from the nearby creek. Preparations were started for dinner including prepping a fire in the kitchen's wood stove.

Our pledge was to leave everything in better shape than we found it. An increase in the size of the already well-stocked firewood supply was one measure of our progress. Most of our time was spent clearing trails of fallen trees, carrying limbs, sawing logs, and splitting firewood.

After a hardy dinner and a cozy fire, it didn't take long before we were ready to call it a night. The kitchen opening was sealed with a piece of door-sized Masonite to keep in the stone fireplace's radiant warmth.

The girls slept downstairs with Mrs. True. The guys slept in the attic loft with Mr. True.

I slept soundly in my sleeping bag until morning's light came in the small window. Kevin was silently motioning me over to it. The ground was covered with a blanket of newly fallen snow. Close in, at the tree-line, were two dozen deer. Some seemed to look longingly at the cabin.

The girls slept less peacefully. Something had been ransacking the kitchen. Upon inspection, most of our two pounds of ground beef was missing. Stashes of it were hidden all around the kitchen. Mr. True moved the furniture, found the animal's access holes, and blocked them.

Learning the Cabin's History

The wide pages of the guest book made for interesting reading. People from all over the world had signed. Many were Appalachian Trail hikers who had taken a detour to visit. The stories of others who had stayed over were fun and enlightening. We learned about the cabin's various quirks, such as our night visitor. It was the resident skunk.

Taped inside the book's cover were clippings about the structure's origin. "Nicholson Hollow" had been cleared and farmed since the 1700's. A "hollow" in Appalachian vernacular is a small, sheltered valley that usually contains a stream.

George Thurman Corbin, age 21, had built this cabin in 1909 for his wife of three years, Bertie ("Nee"), and their two babies. They had two more children here while living by ax, gun, and plow. Nee died in childbirth in their home during the winter of 1924 while George was getting the doctor. In 1932 George spent everything he had, $1,400, to roof the cabin in long-lasting tin. Then in 1935, to build Shenandoah

Park, FDR's administration took his property and home by eminent domain, paying him only $1,400 total. The fields were reforested.

The girls' second night of sleep was even more disturbed. The creature was furious that it couldn't get back into the kitchen. It hissed, cried like a cat, and grunted, but remained scentless.

After we left I was obsessed with sketching Corbin Cabin as if it were the Devil's Tower in the movie *Close Encounters of the Third Kind*. My brain hungered for a return to capture more details.

A Room with a Valley View

The next winter Corbin Cabin was not available. Instead, we stayed in the "Range View Cabin" on the west side of Skyline Drive. Being  a shelter, not a home, it lacked deep history and real windows, but from its doorway there were beautiful views of the distant Blue Ridge mountains, the sunsets, and the twinkling lights of Luray below.

The portage in over the packed snow wasn't far. As we'd done the year before, we devoted ourselves to building up the wood pile. Though it was freezing, we became very hot cutting logs with the two-man cabin saw. We should have noticed the coming cold and the place's exposed construction: a chilling west wind gusted up and through the outhouse constantly.

We went to sleep that night in warm and toasty bunks, thanks to the roaring wood stove. It was a good time to discretely wash and get into the next day's underwear and long underwear. An important camping rule is to never go to sleep in the day's damp clothes.

That morning we were all freezing. The light of our flashlights revealed our breath rising to the rafters. Everyone pulled their knit-hat-covered heads deep into their sleeping bags. Everyone, that is, except for Janice

Pritchard. She braved the chill to get a fire going. She said that the cookware had frozen to the table.

That day we had an easy hike to Dark Hollow Falls until we crossed Skyline Drive. There the popular pilgrimage trail went almost straight down to the waterfall from a small parking area. It was frozen thick with ice. We couldn't stop laughing at our attempts to guide our slide.

At the end we were in awe. Above us, the cascading frozen falls was breathtaking. It had many levels and offshoots. The sunlight revealed the intricacies of this glittering marvel.

The effort to ascend the ¾-mile sliding board took forever. Sometimes we formed human chains using trees as anchor points. That second night, we kept the stove fire burning.

Third Winter Is the Charm

During our return to Corbin Cabin in February 1977, there was already snow on the ground. I deeply appreciated going back to this real home after the previous year's stay in the exposed shelter. The wisdom of the Appalachian common folk was becoming more apparent.

Our hike in was memorable that year. Crossing the loud babbling brook was tricky, especially with a full pack. Its noise drowned out speech. Big Jim and Little Mike had reached a point where they both wanted to hop from their perches to the same round rock. Over the water's roar, Mike yelled, "Don't jump!" but Jim only heard "Jump!" They collided in mid-air, and Mike bounced off into the freezing water. He ran the last mile to the cabin, where he changed.

Our previous "pioneering" experiences had prepared us in many ways. For example, this time I brought our family's big bow saw. Its new blade cut firewood logs more easily than the cabin's saws.

During this trip we visited the primitive grave markers and the remains of nearby cabins built by the relatives of George Corbin. Their bottom timbers were rotting, causing these roofed cabins to slowly sink. It was sad, but it was easier to see construction details. Each log had a pentagon shape whose peak was fitted into a kerf in the log above.

Everywhere the animal tracks in the snow generated curiosity and conjecture. Back behind the cabin were huge footprints. The stride between steps was very large. Some imaginations excitedly jumped to idea of a large, hairy Sasquatch. As I stroked my bearded chin, an idea began to form. (My attempt at cold creek shaving during our first visit had been too painful.)

That evening we had a sumptuous dinner at the cabin's long table. After the dishes were washed, there was a deep pan of rinse water to remove. Janice opened the kitchen's back door, carried it out on the stoop, and pitched the water into the dark. Suddenly, there was a loud high-pitched scream. It was the unmistakable voice of the Corbin Cabin skunk.

At the table we were treated to an unexpected surprise. Mrs. True had hidden candle wax and wicks in the supplies that were ported in. Our candle dipping night turned out to be more fun than expected. With each dip of our wicks, layers of wax built up on our growing candles.

Suddenly, Bruce Mello plunged his whole hand into the molten red wax. He was able to build up layers around his outstretched fingers by repeated dipping. Somehow, we extracted him from his hand-shaped candle, inserted five fingertip wicks, and filled it with hot wax.

Bruce's spontaneity sparked our creative juices. We began sculpting our newly formed and pliable candles. I corkscrewed two candles around a third.

Feeling the Warmth

Everyone cuddled around the hearth fire, sitting on a table bench, stools, and the floor. People were using each other as backrests. We munched on Froot Loops.

I went out to use the outhouse. While enjoying the solitude, I could detect something moving outside. I peeked out the door into the moonlight. A few feet away, a deer was cautiously moving toward the cabin.

My 1977 drawing. Note bow saw, hand candle, and night visitor.

Crouching just outside the outhouse, I couldn't believe all the deer. They were going past me on both sides through the woods toward the creek. My dark sweater with its white shoulders blended well with the other snow-covered rocks. When they moved, I moved.

The cabin door opened, and they froze. Mr. True was on the porch calling me. As he panned the woods with a spotlight flashlight, it was interesting to watch the big doe near me. The light passed over her body, showing her fur in detail. After he went in, the deer swiftly vanished.

Now that my disappearance was causing concern inside, it was time for mischief. Grabbing a branch, I stood behind the chimney. I would only scratch on the shutter while they talked.

My prank caused commotion, but Corbin needed no artificial atmosphere. This year the downstairs had not been disturbed nightly by the skunk. Instead, an apparition was seen carrying a candle up to the loft. Based on various guest book entries, it was determined to be Mrs. Corbin. She was trying to signal to her husband and the doc to come quickly.

Winter turned out to be a great time for these trips. There was no rain, no mosquitoes, and no mud. Also, firewood was much easier to gather, and the fire's warmth was cozy and welcome.

~

Epilogue: Mr. True vividly remembers getting us home from Corbin Cabin that first time. It took two cars to transport all of us and our gear. One car was the True's station wagon, which was left parked just off the highway at the trailhead. The second car was provided by one parent dropping us off while another was coming to pick us up.

In Mr. True's own words: "Another thought on Corbin Cabin. We hiked the four miles out in 12 inches of new snow, and our pickup car couldn't make it from New Carrollton, so we had to all pile into one station wagon and pile packs onto the roof. The snow got deeper and deeper the closer we got to the city. Every time we dropped a kid off, everyone had to get out and push to get us going again, the snow was so bad in Maryland. Many mothers called the Park Service during the blizzard to see if we were OK, and of course no one knew—but we were doing fine!"

Lengthening Strides

"Here's a new outing you might want to try," tall and lanky Mr. True announced to the almost dozen Explorer post members sitting on his living room floor. During these monthly meetings at the True's house, we planned and organized our upcoming outdoor activities. This had made it possible to go caving, rock climbing, pioneering, and more. What was his new idea?

"How about going on a 50-mile hike?" he continued. Many of our outings had included hikes, but they had always been just to reach a destination. In the Boy Scouts, we might hike 12 miles, pitch camp, and then hike another eight. We asked, "How many days would this 50-mile hike take?"

Impishly he answered, "One day," holding up a finger. "It starts at midnight at the C&O Canal's 55-mile marker and ends at the five-mile marker." He enjoyed watching his young teenage audience squirm with our "Impossible! FIFTY miles! Got to be kidding!" reactions.

Appealing to our self-challenging nature, Mr. True stated, "If it's too much for you, just do the warm-up hikes." Then, appealing to our goal-oriented nature, "But everyone who finishes the 50 miles in 20 hours will get an Amos Alonzo Stagg medal." The 5-, 10-, 15-, 20-, and 25-mile warm-up hikes had already been scheduled for consecutive weekends that spring. Like most of our group, I only hiked the last three.

The hikes had been organized by the New Carrollton Hiking and Camping Club since 1974 and were open to anybody. The local warm-up or "conditioning" hikes were amazingly immersed in nature. Though they were in the Washington, DC, area, they were rarely within sight of civilization. Primarily, we were breaking in our hiking boots, lengthening our strides, and building up our stamina. An unexpected benefit was the chance to have casual and deep talks with our peers while enjoying nature. Since I made them in both 1975 and 1976, most descriptions will be of my first-year hikes.

Paint Branch

During the 15-mile Paint Branch hike, we walked northward on the sunlight-dappled trail from near Fletchers Field up to the Colesville area. Because the dense foliage hid any structures, I was surprised when the back of a couple of houses came into view on our right after more than an hour of hiking. More surprising was a white Skyhawk jet parked on our left that was inexplicably abandoned and overgrown. Buzzing small-plane activity above the trees indicated that we were near the tiny College Park Airport.

Type of abandoned jet near College Park Airport

Next, we came upon Lake Artemesia with its big island and pavilion. Later we passed under the Beltway's bridges. Later development has

Current image of Lake Artemesia

encroached on the trail there, especially the interchange of I-95 at the Beltway. Now a southern section has become the popular (but hidden) Prince George's County 3.5-mile Paint Branch Trail. The northern section has become the Montgomery County 2.3-mile, asphalt-paved Paint Branch Trail.

The Mount Vernon Hike

For the start of the 20-mile Mount Vernon hike, we were dropped off near the entirely forested Roosevelt Island in Roslyn on the Virginia side of the Potomac. Brief directions on a slip of paper led us southwards toward the entrance to Mount Vernon. In the bright March sun, there wasn't much shade. We all walked at different speeds. No one viewed hiking as a race; it was all about the journey.

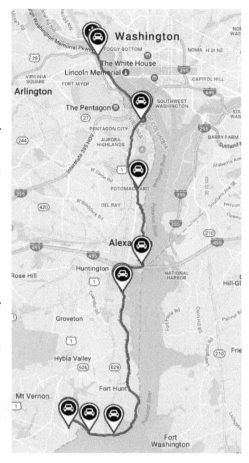

There was a group of longhaired guys in bell-bottom jeans stopped up ahead to refill their canteens. They were having a deep conversation about "Tommy." Curious and naive, I asked, "Tommy who?" Thus, began a "Who's on first" back-and-forth at my expense. Finally, they disgustedly asked, "Don't you know about The Who's movie *Tommy*? (It had just been released that month.)

Most of my memories are a blur, but I remember feeling a little morose that day. It was taking me a while to get over drifting apart from my girlfriend, Janice. She had introduced me to the Explorer post. We had always kept our dating a secret from the other Explorers, not wanting to ruin a good thing. However, during the hike, she acted like I wasn't even there. Seeing her happy in the beautiful sunlight made me even gloomier. We were kids not knowing that losing "our forever love" was just a part of growing pains.

Because the trail was neither marked nor complete yet, at a point where the directions unexpectedly sent us off down some quiet suburban streets, a group of hikers convened. A beautiful longhaired collie surprisingly greeted us. Its dog tag address seemed nearby, so two kids brought the collie home as the rest of us picked our way through this detour.

Along the hike, the planes and the runways of National Airport came into view. At the hike's end, I was disappointed to not even catch a glimpse of Mount Vernon due to its high wall and gate. We waited there to be picked up. Earlier, in 1972, our hike path had been designated a "trail." Nowadays some wooden walkways have been built, making it much more direct. It's become a very popular 18-mile scenic path.

Slippery When Wet

The first year on the Rock Creek 25-mile hike, the rain held off until we were finished. Because you had to pick your way along the sloping and

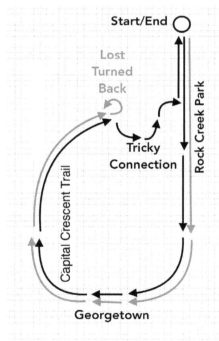

occasionally rocky banks of Rock Creek, it was almost as tiring as the later 50-mile hike. In order to extend the hike to 25 miles long, it was shaped like a hook. We walked southward down the shank through Rock Creek Park until turning onto the C&O Canal in Georgetown. After following the canal's towpath westward, we turned north to hike on what is now called the Capital Crescent Trail.

This part was very tricky, given our minimal directions. Especially tricky was the connection from the top of the Crescent Trail back to the

Rock Creek Trail, where we were to backtrack to our starting point. The first year, everyone managed to find the connection. However, the second year it rained on our ponchos the whole time, making for bad visibility. My friend Robert Cheng and a group of other first-timers couldn't make out that tricky connection. They took the only safe option: they returned the way they came, making for a much longer, almost 40-mile hike.

The Funny Drive Home

Both of these stories occurred a year apart at the intersection of Route 1 and 410/East-West Highway after our 25-mile hikes. The first year, the rain was coming down in buckets as our car full of returning kids drove home northward toward the intersection. We came to a stop behind a line of cars, even though our light was green. People were honking at a long white car that had conked out as it had tried to

Old Pierce Mill, the Taft Bridge over the Rock Creek trail, and the C&O Canal towpath in Georgetown.

cross Route 1 right under the light. With the torrential rain, nobody ventured to help.

Someone in our car pointed out that only we could save the day and move that blocking car. "Teenage power!" we yelled as we exploded out into the rain. Instantly drenched, we ran up and pushed the car as its driver steered it toward a shoulder. We were soaked but laughing as we got back into our car.

The second year, the rain had stopped right after the hike ended. As our Bowie-bound car* approached the same intersection, Robert Cheng suggested that we pull into the McDonald's on the corner. He

was very hungry. As we all ordered our lunches, Robert wasn't sure which of the five sandwiches were better, so he ordered one of everything. We watched him eat a hamburger, a cheeseburger, a fish fillet burger, a Big Mac, and a quarter pounder. Where did all that food go in Robert Cheng's skinny frame?

After the last sips of his drink, Robert said he still felt hungry, so he went up and ordered an apple pie for dessert. Hiking takes a lot more out of you than you realize.

The intersection four decades later is no longer two-lane roads.

Please excuse this story's landmark photos copied from the web. Our views were primarily of trees, glorious trees. They are as difficult to capture on film as the Grand Canyon. Also, to supplement these memories, I used Google Maps and TrailLink to find the trail's current disposition.

---

*It was my red VW. Robert Baer remembers volunteering to ride in its small way-back area. My long-legged brother Jeff sat beside me in the passenger seat. In the back seat were Janice, her friend Beth, and Robert Cheng. My tales of our first year's hikes had convinced him and others to do them with us in 1976.

Fifty Miles in One Day

Because the 50-mile hike began at midnight on a Friday night in late April, I worked ahead in my homework and tried to take a nap after school. It's difficult to sleep when you're ready for a big challenge but must wait. After dinner and a shower, it felt odd to put on the next day's clothes rather than pajamas. Then I carpooled to the rendezvous point at the parking lot of Lamont Elementary School in New Carrollton. It was always fascinating to me that Lamont Elementary was exactly the same as Foxhill Elementary back in Bowie.

Not going directly to the canal start point seemed senseless, but Mr. True said that the mayor of New Carrollton wanted to see us off. He

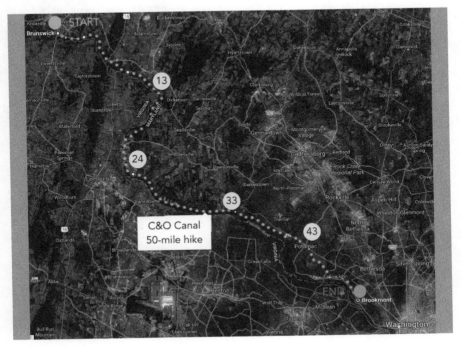

C&O Canal
50-mile hike

also said that if we couldn't finish the hike in 20 hours to earn a medal, we should just get to a checkpoint before nightfall. Standing on a lit part of the school sidewalk, the mayor wished us well. Back in our cars, we drove to the starting point.

~

Most of this tale is from memories of my first hike because it was a time of discovery. Later specifics are from a 1976 award program provided by my friend Robert Baer.

We arrived at the 55-mile marker on the C&O Canal well before midnight. As our eyes adjusted to the darkness we could see puddles in the towpath up ahead. It ran to the right of the canal. The moonlight made it obvious that flashlights were worthless. They and all useless weight were handed over to those who'd be manning the checkpoints. I asked Amy Oosterhout, another explorer, if I could walk with her.

Someone joked, "It's all downhill from here." Sure, we would drop about 150 feet in elevation, but the wide towpath was perfectly level between locks. Each time we passed one of the 25 sets of locks that we'd encounter, the towpath would slope slightly downward. At midnight, about 50 of us started the hike.

After more than three hours of walking, hikers began arriving at the first of the four checkpoints in dribs and drabs. Our arrival time was written next to our name on a clipboard. No need to hang around— we still had 37 miles to go. After refilling my old dented Boy Scout canteen and stocking up on more boxes of raisins, Amy and I were back out on the trail.

Raisin Tossing

We knew that dehydration was our main enemy. The mother of one of the hikers was a very helpful nurse. She recommended vitamin C in the form of raisins to reduce the lactic acid build-up in our muscles. They were the secret to avoiding muscle cramps. During the hike I ate tons of raisins. At first, I'd just dump each little red boxful in my mouth. Then I started throwing raisins in one at a time. Soon I was tossing each raisin 20 feet up and catching it in my mouth without missing a step.

Between times of conversation, our wide, moonlit trail was eerily quiet. The repetitive crunching of our boots on the trail disappeared into our subconscious. Up ahead there was a strange glow and a faint hum. It was too early for sunrise. Unexpectedly, a brightly lit, massive power station came into view across the canal. It was magnificently out of place. During later excited retelling, we learned that it was named Dickerson.

Eventually, light on upper tree branches gave evidence of dawn. The twittering of birds grew in sync with the growing light. Our trail was abruptly invaded by a dozen bespectacled and binoculared strangers. What were *they* doing up at this early hour? I would have thrown raisins at them, but my aim was getting so good that I'd have hit them. Then we saw them quietly showing each other little open books and pointing in all directions. They were birdwatchers, of course!

The Midpoint Checkpoint

At Edwards Ferry, after having walked 24 miles, it was time for a real pit stop. After grabbing my sneakers and new socks, I gladly accepted the nurse's offer for a foot wash. Her rubbing alcohol felt cool on my feet. It was a luxury to be seated. I tried to switch from

my ankle-high boots to lightweight sneakers, but each step was like walking on coals. My tender feet could feel the sharp edge of every stone through the thin soles, so I changed back into my warm boots and soon was back on the trail.

The towpath at Lock 20 looking back westward

Day hikers and bikers became more numerous as the day wore on. Fortunately, the towpath was wide. At the top of one of the ramped lock sections, Amy and I caught sight of her brother, Paul, walking like a zombie. Momentum brought him quickly down the incline. A bicycle had stopped directly in front of him. Lacking the energy to jump aside, Paul grabbed the handlebars and stopped with one long leg on either side of the front wheel. Without a word he simply lifted one leg over and kept walking.

Only Several Hours to Go

At the final checkpoint, with seven miles to go, I felt a second wind. Leaving Amy and her brother, I wanted to see if I could actually walk faster during this last leg. Using the mile markers and my good old Timex watch, it was easy to judge that my pace was faster. At the finish line a small group started cheering when I came into view. It seemed impossible to actually walk 50 miles in one day!

Back at home I walked very gingerly. It would take days for my feet to heal. During the hike I'd lost 12 pounds, mostly water weight. Sleep came quickly, and I slept soundly for 18 hours straight!

"Pomp and Circumstance"

Months later, the mayor of New Carrollton held a low-key ceremony to award us our "Amos Alonzo Stagg" medals. It was held in the top floor of a small two-story cinderblock building about the size of a three-car garage. Before it started, some of the girls were laughing when one of the hikers proudly said to them, "Feel this leg. Does it feel like the leg of a 76-year-old man?"

Hikers completing the 50-mile hike in 1975 (in order of finish): Dick Strafella, Bill Murray, Al Schroetel, Pete Olson, Bob McGinn, Gil Dagg, Dick Richter, Cathy Jones, *Fred True*, James Cooley, Martha Jones, Jeni Weinbach, *David Maxwell*, Steve Keller, Bill Hocking,

Mr. True, Dave Maxwell, and me

Steve Poynter, Ann Brennan, Sharon Midkiff, Robert Dudka, Vera Weinbach, Karla Capps, George Keller, Ed Limberger, *Me*, Nancy Jones, *Paul Oosterhaut, Jim Mello, Rick True*, Barbara Haase, *Bill True, Bruce Mello*, Jean Keller, Bob Baird, Mike Baird, David Dean, *Kevin Slocum, Janice Pritchard, Beth Stark*, Marie Keleher, Linda Rowe, Barry Capps, Chris Lynch, Dave Huffman, Diane Bickers, *Amy Oosterhout*, Diane Liberti, Libby Curry, Lorinda Lawson, Annette Dag, Kathy Wells, Joey Oosterhaut. *(Members of Explorer Post 1286 in bold italic.)*

During the program we also learned that the youngest hiker to finish was—unbelievably—a nine-year old boy. However, being typical teenagers, we had only noticed those we knew on the dark trail at the start. Because we had to prove to ourselves that it wasn't a fluke, some of us hiked the 50 again the next year.

The 1976 Hike

After the experience of completing the 50, it was hard not to tell your friends. Next spring my brother Jeff and two neighborhood friends, Robert Baer and Robert Cheng, tried it. All of them finished the hike. Later, my brother Jeff discovered that the pain in his foot was due to a bone unknowingly fractured in the top of his foot *before* the hike. He even ran the first stretch!

That year I noticed hardly anything else because I was smitten with my girlfriend, Janet Krueger. We had met the previous fall at the two-day/two-night Baltimore Science Symposium. One junior from each high school in Maryland was chosen to attend. She was from Northwestern High in Hyattsville. I couldn't wait to see her again, no matter how long the hike, as she was always delightful company.

At the start of that year's 50 there were 37 people—quite a crowd. There was a group of a few joggers who would finish hours before us hikers. They saw it as simply a "more-than-double marathon." After hiking a distance in the crowd, I winked at Janet, stopped, and pretended to tie my shoe. After everyone passed us, we ducked off the trail. After a while, we came back to find the trail empty. Walking along the moonlit canal, it was like we were the only people on earth.

Robert Baer completed the hike again in 1977. My gaming buddy, John Cook, also hiked it that year and even set the record for hiker completion at 13:38. In 2003, Robert Baer was hit severely by a car in front of the White House. His recovery was helped by the love of hiking he acquired on these hikes.

New Carrollton Hiking Club's 50 Mile Hike, 1976

Hikers	Monocacy Aqudct. 13	Edwards Ferry 24	Violets Lock 33	Wide-water 43	Lock Five 50	Finish Time 50 Mile	total mph
Dick Strafella						11:54 PM	4.20
Ed Jones						11:54 PM	4.20
Norm Whalen						11:54 PM	4.20
Keith Sapack						1:57 PM	3.58
Annette Dag						2:14 PM	3.51
James Cooley						2:14 PM	3.51
Jeni Weinbach						2:14 PM	3.51
Pam Matais						2:14 PM	3.51
Jackie Hoaglund						3:24 PM	3.25
Martha Jones						3:24 PM	3.25
Carl Kronlage						3:50 PM	3.16
Fred True						4:00 PM	3.13
Bill Hocking						4:03 PM	3.12
Jeffrey Stewart						4:40 PM	3.00
Robert Cheng						4:40 PM	3.00
Gordon Stewart						4:41 PM	3.00
Janet Krueger						4:41 PM	3.00
Kevin Sapack						4:49 PM	2.97
Jean Keller						4:55 PM	2.96
Amy Oosterhout						5:30 PM	2.86
Janice Pritchard						5:30 PM	2.86
Brenda Howar						5:30 PM	2.86
Celeste Gervasio						5:37 PM	2.84
Karen Harper						5:37 PM	2.84
Robert Baer						6:08 PM	2.76
Charles Sutton						6:15 PM	2.74
Cathy Masciarelli						6:23 PM	2.72
Denise Burall						6:35 PM	2.69
Mike Baird						7:14 PM	2.60
Robert Baird						7:14 PM	2.60

Here is a spreadsheet of the 1976 hike timesheet data, with the 31 finishers ordered by finish time. Remember, hiking was not seen as a race. This is just to make it easy to see who was hiking together.

In 1980, the Sierra Club took over the long C&O Canal hike. They lengthened it to 100 km (62.5 miles) for some reason and called it the "one-day hike." There have been various DC-area 50-miler hikes since.

Extra Explorer Exploits

Those three years of high-adventure exploring went by in a blur. The outings mentioned in the previous chapters are but the tip of the iceberg. Here are highlights showing some different facets.

One of our early canoe trips was down the wide Shenandoah River. I particularly remember playing "O Shenandoah" on my harmonica when a spectacular panorama opened up.

After that natural beauty, it was shocking to hear that our next canoe trip would be in New Jersey. What struck me during our family visits to relatives in northern New Jersey was its endless elevated turnpike traffic, slogging through the fumes of flame-tipped refineries. We'd often kid Mom about it. She would defend her state as the "Garden State," but to us it looked like all of nature had been paved over.

Conversely, almost a quarter of the state was bypassed by settlement because it had sandy, waterlogged soil. These "Pine Barrens" were a new kind of wilderness to us. Our route flowed eastward through its flat marshes and scrub pines.

The Pine Barrens

It was the total flip side of the state's dense urbanization. We paddled our canoes for eight hours without seeing any buildings, signs, or electric lines. The only evidence of civilization was a small, empty, one-lane bridge that we had to duck under.

One of our endeavors was completely different. At a meeting, Mr. True mentioned that the New Carrollton fair needed volunteers that Saturday, so we arrived bright and early. It was a comfortable, sunny day. At the beginning we were all assigned to the face painting area. After quickly setting it up, everybody went off to help elsewhere, except for Janice and me. We each painted many cute little faces. Their reactions were priceless.

Go West

Most of our trips were westward bound. There were large swaths of nature along the East Coast, but the expansive wilderness lay along the inland mountain ranges. Several times on the way west, we dropped by a very unique store.

It was out in the Virginia country on a small, two-lane road. Along the right side of the road, there was a ramshackle building with a sign that read, "Appalachian Outfitters." It was situated at the edge of civilization, awaiting to equip passing adventurers.

Abandoned shop before parts were relocated
away from Hunter Mills-123 intersection

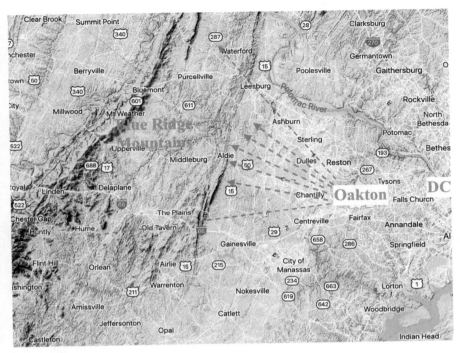

The ranges visible from the store

This was over a decade before the current Appalachian Outfitters was founded and REI came to the East Coast. Back then there was only a large Sunny's Surplus store in downtown Baltimore. Its dimly lit floors were full of old army equipment. Also, our Annapolis Sears had a small selection of Coleman camping items.

Beyond the Appalachian Outfitter's small storefront were rambling wood floors supporting displays chock full of "real" equipment. They had all the latest in climbing gear, tents, sleeping bags, etc. The young store clerks knew their stuff. One time I bought a pamphlet detailing all the Great Falls cliff climbing spots.

Upon getting back to the car, we had a clear view of the mountain ranges where we were headed. Nowadays it's hard to believe that this shop's location in Oakton, Virginia, was out in country in the 1970s.

Westward Highlights

One sunny summer weekend, we stayed at the "Shaw House." Surrounded by rolling countryside, it was built by friends of the Trues, the Holschuhs, for use by Scouting groups.

Out back was a tempting hill. After hiking upward through a steep field of lush grass, we reached the crest to find a beautiful panorama. Here the grass gave way to an expansive, flat rock. Reaching down quickly revealed it was too hot to touch.

That evening there was no moon. The sky was clear. The abundance of brilliant stars was unbelievable. We walked across the field to stargaze from that vista spot, our bare arms beginning to feel cool. We lay down on the broad, smooth surface of that rock and felt its sun-drenched warmth. Then our chills and goosebumps came from beholding the magnificence above us.

Big Devils Stairs

One voyage westward was to Washington, Virginia, to rappel down a really tall cliff. After descending the many Carderock cliffs, we had all become quite proficient. A cliff over a hundred feet tall would be more than twice as fun to swing down. My only worry was whether our rope would be long enough.

Hiking to the base of Big Devils Stairs was tiring because of the many large rock fragments that could easily turn an ankle. To us it was just gray rock. Only a geologist would know that this wasn't the same solid material of the often-climbed Carderock cliffs. According to Mr. True, this Big Devils Stairs cliff is no longer accessible because this area is now blocked off as private land.

Hanging from such a long rope was a thrill. You could weightlessly jump away from the cliff face, let out more line, and swing back to a new landing. It was worth the circuitous hike back up to the top. However, my impatience didn't mix well with approaching that "age of immortal invincibility."

Maybe there was a shortcut to the right. An inviting ledge took me diagonally up the cliff, whose face was like a gently undulating curtain, so it was impossible to see very far ahead. It was easy to kick away any small obstructing rocks.

At two-thirds of the way up, I discovered that about 20 feet of the ledge ahead had been sheared away. Luckily the cliff face above sloped back at about a 45-degree angle. I just had to climb up, over the shear, and then back down to my ledge.

While climbing over, I came across a boulder about the size of a big suitcase. I yelled "Rock!" before reaching out and up to nudge it down the slope. It took more force than expected to pull it away. Suddenly it started moving, and I did too. As I was sliding down the slope I hoped my toes or fingers would find traction before the slope became the vertical shear.

A foot from the edge I stopped and lay there shaking. Then came the thunder and crashing sound of the boulder far below. I slowly climbed over to the continuation of the ledge. Upon making it to the top, I swore to never free climb again.

Along the top of the cliff, Janice had been sitting and talking with Mike. She had her back to the edge with her arms behind her propping her upright. Without warning, the cliff edge collapsed. As she fell over backwards, Mike grabbed her legs. We were both very fortunate that day.

Fall Cabin Camping

In late 1976, Mr. True was able to reserve another PATC (Potomac Appalachian Trail Club) cabin. It was an old moonshiner's cabin called the Davis Mountain Cabin. I don't remember much about it—not even drawing it.

Yet I do remember "planking." We were hiking through a forest with a clear understory. There was no brush, only widely-spaced, huge tree trunks. The ground was sloping every which way and buried

My rendering of the Davis Mountain Cabin

thigh-deep in dry leaves. We moved along ridge lines where the walking was easier because the leaves had been blown downhill on each side.

We came across a weathered, wide plank and noticed that it slid down through the leaves when we pushed it. It had a twisted galvanized metal strap attached to one end. That became the front of our toboggan. It was surprisingly fast. Several of us would lean back behind our "driver," Bruce Mello, as he pulled back on the strap. As the makeshift toboggan wasn't steerable, his job was to yell "tree!" so we could all bail out in time.

What Was the Secret?

These three years of exciting high-adventure exploring gave me something special to look forward to each month. I hoped someday to create the same thing for my kids as the Trues had done for their sons Bill and Rick. At the time, I didn't question how it had been formed or how it worked. You don't spoil a dream with analysis. Some teenagers joined and left over the years, without fuss. Most of us stayed until it was time to leave for college.

Recently, I discovered that our post originated with a New Carrollton Boy Scout troop. The older boys, just turned teenagers, were eligible to be "Explorers." This section of the troop could be more adventurous. In 1974, the Boy Scout organization started allowing girls to join the Explorer branches. The troop posted ads in local papers. Janice and Beth responded to an ad in the Bowie *Blade*. They were the first girls to join.

That Scouting basis made for a good group. Outdoors people are the salt of earth and good company. But it took more than well-grounded kids to make our group click; it was Mr. True running everything in a very low-key manner.

Bill True, me, Dave Maxwell (behind wood), and Amy Oosterhout

At meetings he and Mrs. True encouraged participatory planning. Young teenagers need to be regarded as young adults who are responsible for their actions. We knew that belonging was a privilege. We didn't need to be reminded to reinforce the group dynamics. There was no drama, division, or jealousy. If someone looked lonely, you went to them.

A Low-Key Example

It wasn't Mr. True but Janice who had told me the three simple rules: academics first, no couples, and a probationary period. After several months Mr. True would decide if each new member worked well with the group. I had forgotten about that when, as a meeting ended, I overheard Mr. True whisper my name to Janice. Immediately she told me that I had been accepted and clarified that it was about the probation period.

It was a one-of-a-kind group. All my searches for other high-adventure Explorer posts only turn up one-week camps or vocational preparation groups. Our post was truly "lightning in a bottle."

Hallway High Jinks

Bowie High's halls were witness to many of our pranks during the late 70s. Many people were sharing lockers, which created opportunities for us to surprise friends, usually for their birthday. One time, to surprise Adie Solomon, Doug and I found a scary looking papier-mâché hand and bust. Doug wrote one of his typical punny poems on thick paper.

In Adie's locker, we put the bust sticking up from a hanging coat, making it look like someone was standing inside, facing out. We lifted up the coat's arm, stiffened it with rolled newspaper, and attached the hand holding Doug's poem up high. We carefully closed the locker with the arm ready to swing down.

Trying to look casual, we "happened" to be nearby when Adie turned the locker's combination. Better than expected, the hand swung down into her hand. Adie looked up with shock, and the paper with the poem fell right into her hand. Often, when Adie got pranked, she would blush as red as her wavy red hair, and still politely thank us for remembering. No wonder she was our favorite target.

Build It, and They Will Come

By our senior year, Chuck Ulrich had perfected the ultimate locker surprise machine, a confetti thrower. No, we weren't stupid enough to employ explosives. Chuck simply attached a piece of cardboard to a spring-loaded mousetrap that sat on the top shelf of the target's locker. A fishing line paper-clipped to the locker door would spring the trap only when the locker door was fully open.

This device required a lot of testing while it was "unloaded." First it was too wide for the locker. Then, when triggered, it might just flip but leave projectiles on the top shelf, or direct them straight down to the floor. Confetti was readily available in the data processing classroom. We collected it from the big machines that punched IBM cards.

Finally, it was the morning of Adie's birthday again. It was usually quite a group production to get her locker-mate to grant us access to her locker before she arrived. We might even "coincidentally" be walking the same way down the hall. Would our machine work? The hall was busy with the usual morning crowd.

Adie dialed her combo and opened the tall door. Suddenly, an outburst of confetti flew over her head and even across the hall! Everyone was shocked, then smiled, and joined in singing "Happy Birthday." We tended not to repeat surprise pranks, especially this one, remembering Adie's words after thanking us: "C'mon, guys. You know how tough it is to get confetti out of everything?"

Sorry that this set of anecdotes isn't accompanied by photos. Back in the 70s we couldn't imagine that someday we would all be carrying around battery-powered, filmless movie cameras in our pockets. Even calculators were bigger than your pockets and required a belt-holster, and phones could only be carried as far as their curly cord.

Pranksters Pranked

We weren't always the pranksters; sometimes pranks were played on us. One time, Doug and I were walking down a second-floor hall at the end of the day. We went into a corner bathroom, absentmindedly not noticing anything strange. I think the bathroom door was propped open, as usual.

Doug said something like, "Did you see this?" We couldn't believe that there was a life-size scuba diver in mask, wetsuit, and fins facing out of one of the stalls. It was not a real person, but a mannequin. As we left the bathroom, I had the impression that someone in the hall was watching for our reaction.

The Head-Banger

Another time, in that same hallway, I was walking toward the back of the school with Christel, a girl I was dating at the time. A crowd was gathering in the corridor, leaving us just room to pass by. We could see that the crowd had gathered to watch a fight. During my three years at Bowie I'd never even heard of a fight.

One of the combatants was big Steve Hamrick, a tough-looking guy. He was getting the best of little, wavy-haired Keith Leibermann. Soon, big Steve was able to grab Keith and start swinging him around in circles. When he let him go, Keith was sent flying headfirst into the wall of lockers. With a resonating bang, his head bounced off as he fell to the floor.

With great resilience, Keith got up and again attacked Steve. Again, he was flung into the lockers with a loud bang as his head jerked back. Christel looked up at me with a horrified look. "Aren't you going to stop this, Gordon?" she asked. It looked and sounded like the fight was getting terribly brutal, especially for Keith.

While replying to Christel, I managed to hide my smile and replied, "Why? I'm quite enjoying this." Unlike most of the crowd, I knew Keith was a surprisingly creative comedian. Also, I'd seen the "fighters" together and knew that they were good friends. To Christel, I gave a subtle hint by finally whispering to her, "They're really amazingly good." It really looked like it was Keith's head, not his arm, that bounced off the metal lockers.

Steve Hamrick,
the thrower

Keith Liebermann,
the throwee

The Night of the 44 Rolls

Many of my childhood adventures revolve around one of my friends, Robert Cheng. Here is proof that fact is stranger than fiction.

It all started in eleventh grade when Robert played a math trick on my lovely girlfriend at the time, Karen Cook (no relation to John). Though she was a stellar student, her misconception about "running averages" made her unduly worried about her grades. Anyway, Robert amazed her by having her do a long series of bogus calculations that ended up predicting her shoe size.

One warm night, I brought Karen out on a date to the popular roller-skating rink in Crofton. Afterwards, I convinced her to go on a moonlit stroll around Allen Pond to its romantic island. We walked

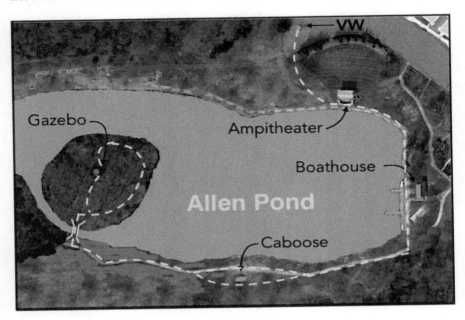

down the gentle grassy slope to the path that ran around the left side of the lake. First, we passed behind the amphitheater's stage and then walked along the short "pier" in front of the small boathouse before heading toward a caboose that was installed on the far side of the lake.

At the time, there were no trees along this path, only grass. We strolled past the restored red caboose. Then the path reached the forested part of the bank and turned toward a short wooden bridge. It led to the densely wooded island. We crossed the bridge and went upward along the island's dirt trail to the gazebo at its peak. From our perch in the gazebo atop this tree-covered island,

we noticed some mischievous activity around my red VW bug in the distance, because it sat glittering beneath a lone streetlight.

The people around my VW eventually left, but later a strange white sedan appeared. It was apparently drawn there by the mischievous activity. Initially, we thought that the white car was a police car, but that thought quickly vanished when it left the parking lot and started driving down the walking path.

Marooned

Trapped on the island, we watched in horror as this odd white car (now definitely not the police) drove off-road along the path toward us. Its menacing headlights seemed to probe for us as it circled the boathouse and then the historic caboose on its way to our bridge. Clutching each other tight, we decided to go down a different trail behind the gazebo. We found a hiding spot off the trail behind a bench. "Swimming for it" was not a real option.

Then we heard a low thumping sound as the car actually drove ONTO the wooden footbridge. Staying out of the headlight's beams, we couldn't figure out how many strangers were searching our island. There were a number of door slams. It felt like ages as horrible outcomes raced through our heads. Our pounding hearts threatened to give us away.

Finally, the car backed off the bridge and seemed to disappear. We crossed the bridge and made a break for it. We had to cover a lot of open ground, only stopping to pause behind the caboose. With no sign of the evil car, we ran to the boathouse. Somewhere along the way, I gave Karen the car keys, telling her that if we became separated, she should take the car and go for help while I distracted them. (Remember, this is BEFORE cell phones.)

As we got to the VW, the white car approached us very rapidly. It seemed to take forever to unlock the doors, clean off some of the decorations on the windshield, and lock ourselves safely inside. (Karen was unfamiliar with my keys, and the VW bug had just been decorated like a homecoming float.)

Gazebo visible on the island during the day

As we took off (with streamers flying), we could see that the driver of the white car was a scary, unshaven man. He will forever remain a mystery. We lost him, but were soon followed by another car, a station wagon.

Seeing the jeering crew hanging out the station wagon windows, I realized that it was my friends who were the mischievous car decorators: Doug, Chuck, and big Sean McGowan. Despite the "punny" poem they had put on my windshield, I was getting increasingly angry as I drove Karen home. Not only had they interrupted a great date, but they had also endangered us by attracting the undue attention of the stranger in the white car. I told them that I wanted to talk to them after dropping Karen off.

A short drive away, I pulled my decorated bug into a side street. The "decorators" stopped behind me and got out of their station wagon, laughing. They started to realize my anger when I proceeded to lock them out of their car. From the street side of the car, one of them clicked a door handle, saying, "Ha-ha, you forgot one!" That was too much; I just exploded, vaulting the station wagon roof and landing on the street, and started flailing away on each of them.

As I calmed down, little did I know that the night was still young. Returning to Karen's house so that they could apologize, I noted how odd it was that, at 1:00 in the morning, her brother greeted us at the door fully dressed and wearing shoes.

Attack on the Cheng house

Karen and her brother then left their house. They were carrying out their long-planned revenge attack on Robert Cheng's house for his "shoe-size math trick." Their toilet-papering raid included leaving a cryptic shoebox behind. Robert, however, thought that their attack must be MY doing.

So, the Next Night . . .

Assembling a motley crew, Robert led a counterattack on my house. Later I learned that when they had thrown all their rolls of toilet paper high into the trees, one of their crew, Dorian Winterfeld, memorably proclaimed, "We need MORE toilet paper!"

A visit to the local 7-11 and many rolls later, it was like a one-yard pastel snowstorm. Multi-colored streamers fluttered from EVERY tree. The heavily mummified lamppost barely shone through its wrappings. I heard that it was a total of 44 rolls of toilet paper. Thus began another humorous series of summer house raids.

Midnight Mischief

Besides being the core of our high school board-gaming club, we four friends (Doug Atkinson, John Cook, Chuck Ulrich, and myself) occasionally planned toilet-papering raids. They were all as different as our creativity could invent. Our raids weren't malignant like the raids of those who "kitchened" random people's houses. They would go around on Wednesday Heavy Pickup nights and fill front yards with the refrigerators, cabinets, and dryers that had been put out for trash.

In contrast, having your house decorated was an honor. You felt neglected if you woke up on your birthday and your house hadn't been hit. It was the thought that counted. Not all raids were planned with the forethought and the secrecy of a surprise party, but ours usually were. Here's a spontaneous one.

One summer night at Doug's, it was getting too dark for us to continue playing basketball. He had a bunch of extra firecrackers, and we suspected that John was at home playing a board game with someone. We came up with a quick plan and headed out in Doug's Pinto.

John's Cape Cod was quiet, but we knew he was home. We tied some of the firecrackers around a candle, lit it, and placed it on his porch. Our delay fuse kept going out. We must have been too noisy going back to relight it. John and his little brother came flying out of their house with water balloons to counterattack, so Doug and I ran back to his Pinto.

Doug and I continued to attempt drive-by bombing runs despite the water-balloon flak. Before each pass, I cranked down the window and lit a match. Doug had to coordinate his driving so we arrived at the target zone just as I lit a firecracker and threw it out the window. Because the Cook brothers were aiming for my open window, I had to crank it up quickly before being hit by their missiles.

When we ran out of firecrackers, Doug and I congratulated each other because we had never been hit. Then we noticed that the back seat was soaked. We'd been shot down.

Doug's House Gets Canned

Along with the usual visual surprise, we thought Doug's house would be a perfect place for a noisy one. The roof of the Atkinson garage sloped downward toward a big, flat driveway. Chuck came up with the idea of using dozens of empty soda cans on the roof and a device that would release them when pulled by a fishing line tied to the front door.

So we all started secretly collecting cans. It was hard to act normal in front of Doug while concealing our planned surprise. At one of our conspiratorial get-togethers, John asked, "So whose ladder are we gonna' use to get on the roof?" Chuck quickly answered, "Don't be silly. I'll just climb up there. You'll see. I have a plan."

The night of our attack, we quietly parked our car near Doug's house. I started toilet papering the front yard trees, while Chuck and John walked behind the garage. Because of a light shining through the utility room window at the back wall of the garage, they had to crouch to avoid detection. John slumped over as he crept, which made him only five feet tall. Ever after, Chuck would kid John about his "Cook Crouch." They carried a picnic table over to the wall, and Chuck used it to climb onto the garage roof.

After moving with great stealth across the roof, Chuck started attaching his small device to the front eaves. (Now you know why we called him "Monkey Man.") Next, he neatly placed the cans, one beside the other, from the eave almost to the roof's peak. Once they were ready to roll, he jumped down.

John and I finished toilet papering the front lawn and got back in the car. Chuck hooked the taut fishing line to the front door and ran to the car just in time. Mr. Atkinson opened the door and had time to say, "What's all this?" when the first can hit with a loud clatter. Then they started landing with gradually increasing speed. After the first dozen had hit with a distinct sound, the rest became a continuous din. It was truly amazing to behold. We drove away smiling and congratulating Chuck. It had been a total success!

On High Alert

One summer's night, our family was watching TV out in the family room. The phone rang and Mom answered. Surprisingly, it was Mr. Atkinson saying, "You're about to be hit." When asked what that meant, he replied, "They just left in a car to toilet paper your house." We all got excited, but decided to make the house look as if we didn't know.

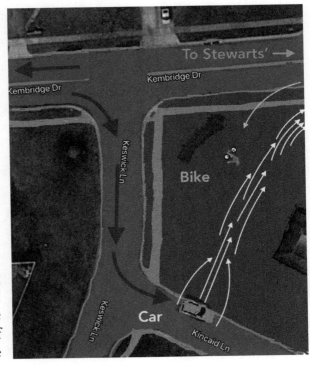

Our best defense was a good offense. Still being in my lifeguard suit, I quickly put on my dark brown windbreaker for camouflage. Hoping to find their car, I put a potato in one pocket and a can of shaving cream in the other. I slipped out of the garage with my trusty, royal-green, three-speed English racer (now called a touring bike) and pedaled away.

Cruising up empty Kembridge Drive by the light of the streetlights, I saw a distant station wagon slowly moving away from me. When they pulled over and turned on their dome light to check a map, I knew it must be them. As they pulled into a driveway to turn around, I knew they would soon be heading toward me. How could I hide and then follow them?

There was a corner lot next to me that sloped down to a peninsula between three streets. That being a long block away from our house, they would surely park somewhere closer. There was a group of low bushes at the bottom of the peninsula. Although I couldn't get very close to them due to a flowerbed, I laid my bike on the grass so that it was partially hidden from their approach. After they passed, I would get up and try to follow them.

As they turned onto the street on the other side of the bushes, I could hear them talking because their windows were down. I lay down beside my bike with all its glittering chrome. Then they turned and parked just 10 yards away with nothing between us!

Watching them get out of the car, I could do nothing but lie motionless. Surely they'll walk around by the street and away from me, I thought, but the four of them walked across the grassy sloping peninsula just a few feet from me and my bike. They were preoccupied with carrying their strings of cans, and they were not expecting a counter-strike.

As soon as they had clanked past, I sprang on their totally open station wagon. They'd even left some toilet paper, so I wrapped the steering wheel. I wrote some of Doug's nicknames on the rear windows, put the potato in the exhaust, and pedaled home the other way around the block.

The hedges along the sides of our yard meant they could only do a frontal assault. However, John and Doug had sent their younger brothers to approach through the hedge along the side of our backyard. These two hobbits, carrying strings of cans, cut through a neighbor's yard and climbed up the slope to our hedges. Their point of breakthrough happened to be next to our white German shepherd's run. Suddenly face-to-muzzle with this white fury, the hobbits fell back, tumbling noisily down the slope.

Meanwhile, on the Main Front

Arriving at the top of my street, I was relieved to find everything quiet. *They must still be moving into position.* I pedaled down the street, cruised up the driveway without being seen, and dismounted beside a roll of garden hose hanging on the sidewall. *My bike must be invisible!*

While watching the street, I quietly took the hose off of its hanger and screwed each of the segments together. Finally, I saw some movement on the driveway. I turned on the water and rushed forward with the hose unwinding behind me. They were right within range as I pointed the nozzle. "Look out—he's got a hose!" they yelled, and ran away.

I ran after them, hoping the water would soon come. Hearing the end of the long hose dragging on the driveway I stopped. I had hooked all the ends of the hose together except the connection to the faucet. Later, when John got back to his decorated car, Doug was already there. For months afterward, John accused Doug of hitting his car. He thought that he had written those things against himself in order to throw off suspicion. Who else could have done it?

Posting Punny Poems

One of Doug's favorite memories of Homecoming was a raid of a different kind. For the Homecoming hall-decorating contest, our high school was always unfair in giving the best hall to the seniors—the one that included the windowed breezeway. Doug, as a junior, was mad that the seniors always won with that advantage. He had an idea to even the odds.

Doug was a prolific punster. He had many ideas for funny poems to write on signs to persuade the judges, but they had to be mounted somewhere out of reach. He came up with an idea to use the breezeway against them. His signs would have the most impact just outside the breezeway windows on the steel columns supporting the third floor above.

However, that meant reaching up over a story and a half on the tall, thin, wide-flange-steel columns. Now, most houses had an 8-foot ladder, or sometimes a 12-foot ladder. Somehow, we borrowed an 18-footer! To help carry and brace the ladder, Doug enlisted John and me. John was a senior and thought it was funny to betray his class.

The high school was deserted, and Doug was atop the ladder taping his last sign. He heard someone tapping on the glass. In the breezeway

windows were the principal, vice principal, and a few other officials. Doug looked over his shoulder and smiled at them while trying to cover accusatory phrases. Luckily, they knew he was a good student and smiled back.

George Peppard on A Team

After climbing down the ladder free from repercussions, Doug smiled and, imitating George Peppard on the *A Team* TV show, said, "I love it when a plan comes together." Our efforts were further repaid when the junior hall won for the first time ever!

Gandalf and the Fellowship

SWAT

It was the mid-1970's, and we were living in a magic time for boardgaming. A second big "designer" boardgame company, SPI (Simulation Publications, Inc.) had risen in the early 70's to challenge Avalon Hill (AH). Having entered Bowie High in 1974, I and a likeminded bunch of mostly 10th graders formed a school gaming group.

John Cook

The most important member of our gaming group was an older, tall 11th grader, John Cook. If our group was the Fellowship, then John was our Gandalf. He was a wizard at reading game rules and teaching them to the group. By the end of my 10th-grade year, our boardgaming club became an official school group, the Strategy Wargames And Tactics club (SWAT—an attempt at sounding cool).

Alexander

At our SWAT club we played mostly historic "counter and hex map" games. One example is Alexander the Great. This game, published in 1971, recreates Alexander's battle in 331 BC on the Gaugamela Plains. He amazingly won, though outnumbered by the vast army of King Darius II. In the 70's, it was considered a fairly easy wargame, playing in only two hours with a brief 24-page rulebook.

Part of the attraction of these historical simulation games was to fill the void in our public education caused by the lack of geography and history teaching. It made me furious when I realized at 14 years

old that I hadn't even been taught the chronological order of the Greek, Egyptian, and Roman Empires. During these games, we made decisions from the viewpoint of historical leaders at critical moments, gaining an understanding that encouraged further investigation via books.

One thing we saw in this game was that the strongest attackers were on the right flank in most ancient armies. This caused the front line to gradually turn counter-clockwise. Shown above is the battle between Alexander's Macedonians (in blue) and the larger Persian army (red). Imagine two fighters dueling by thrusting right-handed swords while defending with left-handed shields. Alexander was able to lead his cavalry in a thrust to the heart of Darius's honor guard before his left flank crumbled.

Gaugamela occurred two years after Alexander's second major battle, Issus. Between those battles, Alexander was able to capture the fortified island city of Tyre, win a battle at Gaza, liberate Egypt (and be declared their pharaoh), and journey through the deadly Libyan desert to a sacred oasis. After all this, he led his well-trained volunteer force of 7,000 against Darius's drafted army of 50-100,000.

The designers of Alexander the Great, Gary Gygax and Don Greenwood, were—and still are—very important to gaming. Their impact is still felt today. We played many games designed by each of them. One game would be Gygax's most famous design, "Dungeons and Dragons."

"In Front of You, You See a 50-foot Corridor . . ."

In 1974, Gary Gygax published the first version of his groundbreaking game, Dungeons and Dragons. Only a few thousand copies of the original game booklets and supplements had been sold when John Cook convinced our SWAT group to give it a try. John, as our Dungeon Master (DM), created a huge, multilevel Dungeon and kept it secret. Drawn on graph paper, he filled its passageways and rooms with traps, treasures, creatures, and puzzles. Anything was possible.

D&D introduced a totally new genre of gaming, which would later be called the "role-playing game" (RPG). During D&D games, players are encouraged to take on medieval-fantasy roles. As a group, they explore a hidden dungeon labyrinth, imaginatively created by one of the players. Rather than imagining you're a commander directing groups of people, you imagine yourself as one character in a group. The journey is emphasized over the destination.

The medieval fantasy setting frees your imagination, encouraging you to be theatrical. Self-conscious of "performing" in Mr. Haworth's classroom, we played this new D&D game only at every other meeting, in the public library's private meeting room. Being mostly serious introverted types, it wasn't our nature to dramatically speak like fantasy characters. We treated D&D more as a group trying to survive and solve John's imaginative puzzles.

To begin the game, the exploring players would roll dice to determine their individual character's abilities: strength, intelligence, charisma, dexterity, etc. We would sit in a group of chairs facing our DM, who sat behind his table full of manuals, charts, and his hidden, hand-drawn dungeon plans. In our first ventures into his dungeon, we'd all either hit dead ends or fall into his traps. John was a fascinating storyteller and rolled his percentile dice to resolve our various attempts.

Ten-Foot Pole

Soon we learned to travel along the dungeon's 10-foot-wide corridors in somewhat of a formation. All of our characters had backpacks full of essentials, including torch materials and the ubiquitous 30-foot rope. One of us would be holding a 10-foot pole out in front of the group to warn us of invisible gelatinous cubes. Tapping the floor in front of us also warned of trap doors. Fighters (dwarves and men) kept swords drawn. Elven archers readied their bows.

Most of our best fighters were in the front, but one always guarded against attacks from behind. Magic users stayed in the middle, along with someone mapping our understanding of the dungeon. However, a lower dungeon level had moving walls; even our chalking them was of little help in our mapping. The players who rolled high in dexterity would search the walls on either side for secret doors.

The characters more likely to have great dexterity were called "half-men" in this first edition. John explained that they were Hobbits, but this word was copyrighted in Tolkien's work. In the hugely popular 1977 version of D&D, Gygax changed the name to "Halflings." Millions of this later-refined '77 edition were sold. Currently, D&D is recognized worldwide. It not only created a whole genre of role-playing games, but also spawned medieval reenactments, Renaissance festivals, etc.

After many adventures, we'd accumulate inside jokes and pun-filled parodies. "You see a large wooden door. Behind it you hear shuffling noises." We kick open the door. "Inside you see a 30-by-30 room with four Orcs playing poker." We couldn't take D&D seriously. I never imagined we'd meet its creator.

SWAT

Bowie High Was Big Enough to Form a Core

Somehow, among the three thousand students who overflowed the three grades at Bowie High, we gamers found each other. The one-hour open lunch probably enabled our core group to form. John Cook, a year older than the rest of us, somehow knew more new games of all types than anyone. He found most of our unique new games. When we got around to Dungeons & Dragons, he was our Dungeon Master. Besides John, three others formed our core group.

Doug Atkinson

Doug Atkinson, having spent some years overseas in England's superb schools, had a much broader view of history. For instance, when I mentioned my wargame between German and Russian tanks, Doug casually replied that he was also interested in the "Eastern Front." I'd never heard that term before. My history and geography education was almost nonexistent.

My contribution was mainly organizing the club's game times and location. At first, we met during open lunch in a willing teacher's classroom, eating while we played. Because it was during the lunch hour and on makeshift tables, only a few turns could be played.

Me

Some of us began subscribing to an amazing monthly magazine called Strategy and Tactics by SPI (Simulations Publication). Each issue included a quick two- to three-hour game along with fascinating articles on the game's topic.

Games and magazines would be shared among us, but similar to the way diplomats are withdrawn before a war, we sometimes quietly requested the return of borrowed materials weeks before a toilet paper raid was launched on someone's house.

The fourth person in our gaming and toilet-papering quartet was Chuck Ulrich. Chuck was more interested in ship-to-ship combat. The always-resourceful John Cook taught our growing group a

multiplayer space-combat game that had us moving our space ships along the classroom floor and measuring distances with rulers, but Chuck really wanted to-scale historic naval battles that required a bigger room. We also needed longer than an hour to game.

Chuck Ulrich

Fortunately, the public library next door would allow us to meet in the large meeting room twice a month, but only if we were an official school group. We were outgrowing our informal open lunch hour sessions and needed scheduled meetings of more than an hour. We needed to become official.

So How Was SWAT Formed?

In the beginning of my 10th-grade year, I heard a request for volunteers to be SGA (Student Government Association) homeroom reps. This thankless job involved learning Robert's Rules of Order, attending monthly SGA meetings, and reporting the meeting's major points to your homeroom. Being curious, I volunteered. I ended up reporting to three homerooms due to the lack of volunteers.

At the SGA meetings, I was surprised to learn that all the student groups, (except sport teams, band, and drama) were actually run by students. The groups' teacher-sponsors merely graded papers while students met in their rooms. Even our "open lunch" was the result of the student protests and petitions organized by our previous SGA. They had stopped the county school system from implementing a plan to have lunch periods after every class period, including the first!

From the SGA I learned the three things needed to create an official school group: 1) A teacher willing to sponsor us and be present in their classroom while we met; 2) A constitution, including bylaws for the group; and 3) An SGA presentation and resolution passed during an SGA meeting. Some school clubs were less substantial than ours, so I figured we had a chance.

Back at our gaming club, we discussed our get-togethers: how often, how long, and where. Among the History teachers, as most games dealt with history, someone suggested Mr. Haworth and got his approval. We decided not to bother with dues, membership, or any other tedium; we were open to anyone who came; and we always had more than enough games to share.

The most important decision was our group name. This was long before "BoardGaming" became popular. Besides, "B G" was hard to put in a cool acronym, and it HAD to be an acronym. The Strategy and Tactics magazine was popular in our group at the time. Most of our games were historical simulations but were categorized as "wargames" (though some dealt with politics or resources). The show SWAT was popular and tough-sounding, so we came up with "Strategic Wargames And Tactics."

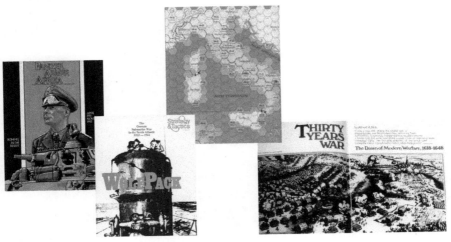

Some of our favorite SPI magazine games during high school:
'73 PanzerArmeeAfrika, '74 Wolfpack, '75 Punic Wars, '76 Breitenfeld (1618–1648)

After writing up our constitution, I created an SGA resolution that was sure to gain approval. Per Robert's Rules, it had many pleading and convincing "Whereas" clauses and the final "Therefore Be It Resolved" clause. After the SGA approval, our SWAT club started meeting after school every other Thursday. Our location alternated between Mr. Haworth's classroom and the public library.

In the Library

In the public library's spacious room, Chuck and Doug could recreate WWI naval battles to scale using finger-long cardboard ship counters that started over a hundred feet apart. Using tape measures, detailed charts, and many die rolls, they recreated the conditions of many important battles. To find information about ships that weren't included in the game, they researched their characteristics at the Library of Congress. Not surprisingly, Chuck later joined the Navy.

The following 1976 and 1977 yearbook photos of our SWAT membership don't tell the whole story. Attendees would come and go throughout the year, excluding our core quartet. All four of us were at most gaming sessions until John graduated in '76. As our game teacher, he was sorely missed. We used to say that as soon as we became good enough to beat John, he would introduce a new game. One game we could never beat John at was "Ace of Aces," where players use flipbooks to dogfight in WWI biplanes.

1975-76 SWAT club, first row: Mr. Haworth, Tom Devlin, me, Michael Kress, Chuck Ulrich; second row: Mark Chertok, Mark Nacewicz, Unidentified, Leonard Ruvinsky, Robert Cheng, Unidentified, John Rosser, John Dagirmanjian

1976-77 SWAT club, standing: Jeff Brown, Jody Austin, Gordon Cook, Chuck Ulrich, Mark Bremer, Bill Cooper, Lee Poloway, Tom Hamill; seated: Doug Atkinson, Tom Devlin, me, Mr. Haworth

Game Con Origins

In 1975 John Cook informed us that one of our favorite game companies, Avalon Hill (AH), was holding something new to the United States, a "boardgaming convention." Because AH was located in Baltimore, the convention was to be held there, at Johns Hopkins. This first convention was called "Origins" by its organizer, Don Greenwood, because he saw it leading to bigger things.

Don Greenwood

Though we missed the first Origins, the next year, Origins II would also be held in Baltimore. After 1976, it would move to a different U.S. city every year. Being the last time it would be within driving distance, we knew it was now or never. Personally, I couldn't imagine a busy convention about our studious and introverted hobby. Because of my lifeguarding job, I could only attend one day of the three-day convention.

"Love, Like Fortune, Favors the Bold"

After John, our club's second-biggest gamer was Doug Atkinson. He and John had been collecting an army of hand-painted fantasy miniatures. Doug was far more courageous than I to get involved in the three-day convention. It amazed me that he was actually entering some of the convention events.

Visiting Origins II

Walking through the outdoor stands at Origins II on that sunny summer day, I was surprised at the number of new games being demonstrated and sold. It was hard to predict which of the games for sale had any potential. I splurged a total of $11 on the mini-games "Stomp" and "The Awful Green Things from Outer Space."

One game booth had a monitor up under the edge of its canvas pavilion. It was showing a stop-action movie of a hex-covered map. Working my way through the crowds, I saw blue counters marching on and forming a circle to the sound of horses galloping and trumpets blowing. Then an even greater number of red counters filled the rest of the screen. One by one the blue counters exploded, leaving a burn mark in their hex on the map. Noticing that the televised game was titled Custer's Last Stand, I wondered why they wasted so much effort.

The most memorable part of Origins II was dropping by the games that Doug had signed up to play.

Doug's Battle over Castle Hill

Doug Atkinson

The first was a refereed miniature game. Neither player could see the other's units except for the figures that had an unobstructed line of sight between them. Each player had a screened copy of the map to move their army on during their turn. A referee would judge if opposing units could see each other at the end of a turn. If they could, he would place the "seen" figures on the central landscaped playing board.

The crowd watched this main playing board as the battle progressed. It was a table about the size of a 4 x 8 sheet of plywood. The armies started (hidden) at either end. In the middle was a big, eye-level tall, papier-maché mountain sparsely covered with trees. This misshapen mass filled the center of the board like a steep pile of laundry, leaving only several inches of flat board on each side of the mountain.

Atop this central mountain was a beautifully detailed castle. The whole setup was eye-catching, but the steep slopes weren't really made for miniature figures. Most people's armies were composed of cavalry. To make it fair, each player's army was limited to a total point value, say 800. The referee had a book of each unit's cost. Doug was quick to see the best solution and thought outside the box. He put most of his points in one basket. Within the point total, he chose one wizard with the expensive powers of invisibility and fireball throwing. His remaining points became several regular characters to use as decoys.

Outnumbered?

No one except Doug and the referee knew what he was up to. During the first turns, both sides of mountain were devoid of figures because neither army could see the other. Then the crowd's interest grew, as some of each side's figures appeared peeking around the mountain on Doug's right flank. It looked like an unfair fight. Doug only had a few characters facing the opponent's charging, closely spaced cavalry. The cavalry included about 60 beautifully painted knights, elven archers, and dwarves.

Between the base of the mountain and the edge of the table, the cavalry was crowded as it entered the long, thin flatland. The next turn saw the cavalry advance and Doug's footmen retreat. Everyone was surprised when the referee announced, "Now, the combat phase." How could anyone be within range?

Suddenly, the front quarter of the cavalry became victim to a fireball. This naturally caused much consternation. The next turn saw another destructive fireball as the remaining mounted archers fired blindly. Soon the battle was over and Doug's strategy was revealed. It was a total roasting.

"To the Left of Your Path Is a Dangerous-Looking, Black Lake"

After cruising around the convention some more, I dropped by to watch another of Doug's games. This was a new game that had just come out in somewhat of a prototype version two years before: Dungeons and Dragons. Onlookers whispered in the hushed tones of a golf match. Doug and the other explorers had reached a dead end after carefully hiking along the banks of a deadly lake. They could see only two choices: a shallow cave and a treacherous, low bridge across the lake.

Another onlooker whispered to me, "Can you believe that the Dungeon Master is *the* Gary Gygax!" Unbelievably, the lively DM was the inventor of Dungeons and Dragons. He had created a very novel game system that would unleash the story-telling creativity of millions of future DMs and explorers. However, trying to DM for a group of strangers at a convention was proving difficult.

Gary Gygax

Doug was leading this group because of his familiarity with our D&D sessions with John Cook. But John designed dungeons with many directions to explore. The only thing Doug's group managed to find at this juncture was a "spacesuit" inside the shallow cave. They had also found one sword, but only after over an hour of exploring.

A Dead End

Finally, Doug became impatient, saying, "I put on the spacesuit, grab the sword, and run across the bridge." Gary, the DM, said, "You made it to the center," then rolled the dice and continued, "A lake monster grabs you in its tentacles and pulls you under." Doug's fighting was useless; Gary declared him dead.

Doug called shenanigans. Gary said that he had a sketch to prove it. Unbelievably, he pulled out a detailed sketch of tentacles wrapping around a guy in a spacesuit holding a sword while being pulled from a bridge. Doug's character was dead; anyway, he'd had enough. John's open-ended creativity grew in our esteem.

Aftermath

Nearly 40 years later, in 2015, I attended the World Boardgaming Championship (WBC) convention organized by the same Don Greenwood. Don had run WBC since 1999, and this was my 14th year. Before WBC, Don ran Avaloncon for years in Baltimore.

Don Greenwood (at podium) at WBC 2014 announcing the board's decision to move to Seven Springs for WBC 2016. The board of directors is seated, facing the audience.

By 2015, WBC had grown to nine days long and attracted gamers from 17 countries and almost all 50 states. It hosted over 140 different game tournaments by using volunteer "game masters" (who ran each tournament) and a "survival of the fittest" game-selection process. I played in the PanzerBlitz tournament every year even though the game was invented in 1970.

For its first five years, WBC was near Baltimore in Hunt Valley. The next 10 years it was in Lancaster, Pennsylvania, in the huge Host Hotel. But the Host was deteriorating; we had to move. After our successful move to the Seven Springs Resort near Pittsburgh, Don Greenwood decided to retire. He left a very qualified board of directors to continue doing the job that they had been gradually taking on over the years.

Gary Gygax Gone

In 2008, the sad news of the death of Gary Gygax spread quickly. Many of the millions deeply touched by their D&D experiences wrote tributes on blogs and Facebook, in magazines, etc.

His novel concept enabled many to enjoy exploring imaginative storytelling together.

Today

It felt like we were truly living in *the* golden age of boardgames in the 70s. But in 1992 a new thing called the "World Wide Web" made everything in the world more accessible. One country—Germany—had been making a treasure trove of boardgames. Its culture of producing and enjoying imaginative and new boardgames was discovered. The Internet enabled the world to easily experience German games.

One of these, Settlers of Catan, was introduced to the United States in 1995 and caught on like wildfire. That same year it won Germany's "Spiel de Jaures" (Game of the Year), which is equivalent to the Oscar awards in the U.S. By 2015, more than 22 million copies of Settlers of Catan had been sold in 30 different languages (per *Wiki*). Soon, many other countries had designers aiming for the SdJ award.

In 2000, BoardGameGeek (BGG) became an international gaming website. In 2016, its database listed more than 84,000 games by over 23,000 game designers, and that year it again hosted the largest international Secret Santa in the world, with over 3,000 participants. Over my past years in it, I've sent anonymous presents to Australia, New Zealand, South Korea, Spain, France, Netherlands, England, Germany, Denmark, Canada, and the United States.

Modern jobs involve isolation at computer stations. To compensate for the long hours spent facing computer screens, more and more adults are discovering the interactive play of face-to-face board games. "High tech" needs "high touch." Could we now be living in "*The* golden age of boardgaming"?

Postscript

On Nov 8, 2016, Doug recounted the following: "At Origins II, John and I qualified for the finals of the AH 'Speed Circuit' racing game (turn based). We were given a new race course 'Grand Prix' map to study and over lunch figured out the perfect groove for a lap: you could not be passed if you led from that position. So we picked our car stats to guarantee we would both be in the front row. I went riskier, taking a

1/6 chance at crashing on my first turn. I survived that turn, John fought off another guy to get into groove one turn behind me, and we finished the multiple-lap final 1-2.

"Apparently, nobody else had analyzed the new map much, and their more traditional car builds were unable to catch us. It was funny watching a perfect strategy come through in a 'national' final. Naturally I didn't tell John I was going one step further and taking a slight risk of crash, but we both knew that other car stats were unimportant compared to getting into the perfect lap pattern. We told the moderator/ref about the pattern during the race, once we could not be caught."

John recalls winning the "Ace of Aces" at Origins II.

Driving Dogfights

What led us to use our cars like biplanes? This is how it happened.

Adie Solomon suspected we were going to "hit" (toilet-paper) her house for her birthday. So she told us that her dad didn't like toilet papering. Also, that her pet rock would stand guard. (The Pet Rock craze was big during the last half of 1975.) This challenge fueled our creativity.

Doug invented the plan to "sign" her lawn. He, Chuck, and I came up with many funny ideas for white poster-board signs. Besides happy birthday wishes, we wrote inside jokes, poems, "for sale," math problems, pet rock challenges, etc., then attached them to sticks. I remembered a flat boulder I had seen at a construction site, which would be perfect to overcome her pet rock.

On the night of the raid, we all met and climbed into my red VW bug and headed over to get the boulder. It was about the size of a spare tire and took all three of us to lift it. As gingerly as we could, we placed it on top of the VW's front luggage compartment. Even though we drove slowly, the extreme weight caused the front wheels to occasionally brush against the fenders. Luckily it wasn't far to Adie's.

We quietly placed the signs all over her yard first, saving the boulder for last. Trying to carry it silently was comic. Even though we placed it gently on their concrete porch, the thud sent reverberations through the slab that alerted the Solomons, so we ran for the car to make our getaway.

Mr. Solomon opened the front door as we were almost ready to drive off, but he couldn't open the screen door with our boulder in the way. Later, Adie told us that he just wanted to invite us in for hot chocolate.

By the time we got back to where Chuck and Doug had parked their cars, it was late. Under the glow of the streetlights, the lanes were as deserted as a ghost town. Before driving our separate ways, Chuck and I decided to play a joke on Doug. We would tail him. Soon he caught on and tried to lose us. Then we each took turns as the chased car. Thus "car dog-fighting" was born.

Shake Him Off Your Tail or You're a Goner

To understand our game, you must remember that we were all avid boardgamers. Some of our games were about World War I aerial battles. For instance, before John graduated, he would play us in the flipbook game, "Ace of Aces." Once he got on our tail it was impossible to shake him no matter how we maneuvered. He always won.

 Being fascinated with these young aviators, we devoured books about them and their planes. Like us, they were at the age when your superb agility and awareness make you feel invincible. Because WWI was a time of great innovation, each type of plane had very different handling characteristics.

Likewise, our three compact cars had different capabilities that we discovered through play. Chuck's pale gunmetal-blue, boxy, foreign car was a good all-around craft like the SE-5A biplane. The lack of blind spots, plus Chuck's ever-attentive eagle eye, gave him an advantage during searches and a general heightened awareness.

You might wonder if we were worried about the police while speeding around the Bowie streets in the middle of the night. Back then, quiet Bowie was merely served by the county police, and they were only seen driving to work in the morning and coming home again in the evening. Besides, there weren't ANY cars other than ours on streets during those hours, not even parked cars.

Doug's Turn

Doug's yellow Ford Pinto had a very wide stance and low center of gravity. That made it quick to turn, like the nimble Sopwith Camel biplane. His favorite evasive maneuver required him to find a large "turnabout."

The drop-off circle in front of Tulip Grove School was his favorite. It circled around a large, flat field. We would try to stay on his tail, but he would take the curves as fast as he could. After each lap, Doug would be further ahead. My narrow Bug would almost careen up onto two wheels as it struggled to keep up.

When Doug had gotten a half lap ahead of us, he would take off in another direction. We tried to track his various twists and turns down the empty Bowie streets. When he had lost us, he'd pull far up in a driveway, turn off his lights and engine, and duck down in the seat. He thought it would take forever for us to find him.

However, in a few seconds we'd be flashing our lights at him. Doug wondered how we always caught him so rapidly. We never told him how. When he scrunched down, he left his foot pressing the brake pedal. The glowing brake lights made his Pinto easy to spot.

My Climbing Escape

When we were in a hilly section like Tulip Grove, I would volunteer to be the next victim. Even though my '68 Bug had a small, air-cooled engine, its lightweight chassis and high-torque gear ratio made it excellent for

climbing hills. It was like the quick-climbing Fokker d7. Once I arrived at the base of the hill on Trinity Drive, I would slow almost to a stop. That would put my pursuers in a low gear and at a disadvantage.

As I worked the clutch pedal and stick shift through the gears, my little bug was chugging up the mountain. It wasn't super fast, but it was faster than they were. Then I'd bank wide to make a right-hand turn up Tarragon Lane. Before me, the branches of the row of ancient tulip poplar trees scratched the night sky. This trajectory would send  me up over the town's colonial Belair Mansion, but back to reality.

Now, which street had another red VW in a driveway that might throw them off?

Pageantry and Spirit

It wasn't until my senior year that I became more involved in our high school's Homecoming. During my sophomore year, like most 10th graders I was more interested in learning how to best navigate the labyrinthine school, adjusting to the idea of an hour-long "open" lunch, and practicing parallel parking in the family car. As a junior, I dressed up for the Spirit Week days. On "mismatched clothes day," even some of the teachers would wear funny combos. On "school colors day" there would be a lot of people in burgundy, white, and navy blue.

Also during my junior year, I learned that the Homecoming dance wasn't just a good excuse to ask a girl out. It was a chance to go inside the prestigious Senior Lounge, where the dance was always held. Unlike our cavernous cafeteria, it had carpeted floors, a low ceiling, and unpainted brick walls. Rather than eat lunch with the riffraff on long benches in our glaring echo chamber, seniors ate at round tables in individual chairs. These Fall Homecoming dances were very informal compared to all the fancy spring prom traditions.

Word of Mouth

In the crisp October of 1976, I heard that there was going to be a get-together to build the senior float. I dropped by out of curiosity. It was two weeks before the Homecoming Saturday, so I figured that they must need many worker bees to do the finishing, like in the Rose Bowl parade. They had obtained a long flatbed trailer, but when I got to the house to start working, that was all they had—not even an agreed-upon design.

A group of Homecoming float builders; I'm standing, far left.

Not being part of the "in crowd," I was curious to see how a float was built. A couple dozen of us in jeans and jackets milled around while one person worked. They would turn down offers to help. High school kids were not very good at delegating, especially when no one had experience at building a float. Ours ended up being a simple trailer full of cheering juniors holding big signs with "Class of 77" on them. During the get-together I did learn about the Homecoming Saturday festivities.

Two decades later, I'd have these moments of discovering classmates I hadn't known. One time, I met the mother of one of my daughter's good first-grade friends. We were not only surprised that we were in the same graduating class, but also in this same yearbook photo. She is next to me leaning forward.

Another Spirit Week tradition was the Friday afternoon "Powderpuff Football Game." The bleachers were filled with students let out early to watch the senior girls versus the junior girls. However, the "cheerleaders" stole everyone's attention. They were junior and senior guys acting like comic cheerleaders while sporting dual balloons under their T-shirts.

During the Saturday football game halftime, the winners were announced for the hall decorating and float competitions.

Car-avan

Early on that Saturday, students gathered in the school parking lot to decorate cars. Soon a long conga line of about six-dozen honking cars left the school and slowly meandered through Bowie. To cheer at people, we kept the sliding door on the right side of our VW bus open. Somewhere in the Meadowbrook section, a couple of us were hanging out the door. We didn't see the car in front turning left. Soon the turning top-heavy van was on two wheels and tilting over on us, so we let go and landed running. We jumped back in once the bus righted.

Along the way we passed houses that had been toilet papered with big numbers as part of the decoration. They were football players' houses with their jersey numbers. We also passed some caravan cars that had dropped out due to fender-benders. Many a family car bore scars from this vehicular caterpillar of teenage tailgaters. Next, I went to the parade preparations that were starting in the Belair Bath and Tennis pool club's parking lot.

The booming of the big bass drums could be heard a half-mile away. Getting closer you could hear the staccato of snares and high lilting melodies of flutes. All the nearby streets were lined with parked cars. Participants and onlookers were drawn in by all the preparation commotion.

The Senior B

The large wooden "senior B" arrived in the back of a pickup truck. Someone volunteered several of us senior guys to guard the B against any last-ditch effort by juniors or sophomores to steal it. We supported it during the parade in the back of the pickup. Arriving at our school, we proudly carried it to the senior section of the bleachers.

All year long, the seniors were required to display the B in a public location and dare the other classes to steal it before Homecoming. Usually it was hung high on a barn roof or billboard. There was a story of the B on top of the house of star running back Don Carillo, who lived in a country-clubber. A group of juniors tried unsuccessfully to grab it one evening.

Throughout the game there was much to cheer about. That year our Bowie Bulldogs were the county champs. No visiting team was going to spoil our Homecoming. Many of our high

Scott Weikle, me, Doug Atkinson, and Greg Donberger with the B

school players had been on my team, back when I was playing Belair Boys Club football. They were a tough and scrappy lot. From experience I realized how much effort, time, dedication, and teamwork was required to perform at that level.

At halftime we were awed by another Bowie team that performed at an impressive level: our precision Pom Pom Girls. Like the football players, they started practice during the summer, weeks before school started. With their white cowboy hats and boots, our Poms were better than the Dallas cowgirls.

The wool uniforms they wore were wiltingly warm. They marched in the May Preakness Parade in Baltimore. They also marched in the city's Fourth of July parade, which was a hot mile and a half through town. During the school year, they often practiced after school until after the activity bus left. This meant an hour-long hike home for many of them.

We were proud of our Poms, and not only for their artistic creations. Out-of-town friends and cousins often mentioned our incredible bevy of beautiful Bowie babes.

Speaking of Gorgeous Girls

No Homecoming halftime would be complete without a Homecoming court. The 11 prettiest Bowie girls and their proud fathers were brought forth. The girl with the most student votes was announced as our Homecoming Queen and presented with a bouquet.

HOMECOMING COURT

Kathy Parezo — Soph.
Patsy Myhra — Jr.
Beth Terrill — Sr.
Cathy Hamet — Sr.
Andi Cottrill — Sr.
Kathy Chromy — Sr.
Stephanie Santos — Sr.
Kelly Ormiston — Sr.
Cherie Conover — Jr.
Chris Davis — Soph.

After our football victory and spontaneous celebrations, everyone went home to prepare for that night's Homecoming dance. A couple of weeks later I took Janet to her Homecoming dance at nearby Hyattsville's Northwestern High. Bowie was the visiting team and "spoiled" their Homecoming by winning. However, during the dance they showed an impressive movie of their float's creation and operation. They had built a Rose Bowl-quality float covered with crepe-paper flowers. It had a big operating bulldozer that drove forward and pushed a bulldog back into his doghouse.

Playing the Straight Man

Stories about "being a morning announcer" tend to draw the most interest from other Bowie High alumni. High on the wall of every homeroom was a public address system (PA) squawk box. You had to really pay attention if you wanted to hear all the announcements. The announcers were anonymous. The whole system was mysterious.

Homeroom

We were assigned to the same homeroom for all three years. Homerooms were separated by last name. I thought my "Stewart" last name might put me among S, T, and U students, but in a class of 1,000, not even all the S's were together. We weren't even half of the S's.

The first thing each morning in our homeroom, the announcements started, as always, with, "Good morning, faculty and students. Please rise for the pledge to the flag." I began to get up when I noticed everyone else was staying seated, even the teacher, Ms. Meador. So, bending to peer pressure, I stayed sitting also. It bothered me. Didn't anyone respect the symbol of our country that had been defended by so many lives? Standing was but a small reminder that "freedom isn't free."

The next day I stood for the pledge, silently and non-judgmentally. No one else rose for pledge in my homeroom except for me. For some unknown reason, after a few months, other classmates started joining me, a few at a time. By the end of 11th grade, more than half of my homeroom was standing for the pledge.

At the end of 10th grade, our board-gaming bunch had become big enough to form an official group. I wrote its constitution, convinced Mr. Haworth to be our faculty sponsor, and got it approved by our SGA.

Then I had to learn how to submit an announcement request. Club presidents simply filled out a small quarter-sheet ditto form with what the announcer was to say that week. Every morning the announcer would read, "The board gaming club will meet this Thursday after school, in room 015," for example.

Surprise Appointment

At the end of 11th grade, Ms. Meador, my homeroom teacher, asked me to be a morning announcer during my senior year. Apparently, she had a role in the selection process. However, this time there would be three announcers: Mike Krasney, Jeff Youmans, and me.

Jeff and Mike turned out to be mile-a-minute, natural comedians. Although I was told I was chosen for my voice, it soon became clear I would be the straight man to keep those two under control. As if that were possible.

Our "Studio"

The three of us sat behind a built-in counter in a tiny cinderblock room in the school office area. In front of us, on the wall, was an impressively large switchboard, which allowed us to communicate with any room. Mike and Jeff sat on either side of me. The heavy silver microphone could be slid back and forth, or we just leaned in toward it to talk as we pressed its "mike on" button.

We'd all get there early and divvy up the couple dozen announcements. The date on the wall calendar would be checked, and we'd make sure whose turn it was to say the opening "pledge to the flag." We would close the room's heavy soundproof door. Then the fun would begin.

The Fun

There was lots of time before the schoolwide warning bell. A few minutes later would be the "start of homeroom" bell, which was our cue to officially start. Each day, due to our early arrival, we proved the maxim that idle hands are the devil's workshop.

One fun thing we did was making sound effects that only the three of us could hear. This could range from impersonations, to singing, to imitating machines. One that we perfected was imitating a war correspondent.

Mikey

Jeff might flip up the switch to listen to the rumbling boiler room. "Hear those tanks moving into position?" Then Mike would add in the data processing room's staccato of typing and excitedly mention the machine gun fire. Finally, we'd take turns cupping our hands over the microphone to make the sounds of bombs dropping and explosions while one of us dramatically narrated.

Jeffy

We had only one immediate fear: the switch that sent our playing out to the whole school. And Jeff's acting could get us to fall for his trick every time. Reaching out for the switchboard, Jeff would pretend to turn off a switch. With a seriously worried look, he would say, "Did you know the 'All Call' button was on?" Mike got a really worried look on these occasions.

Gordy

Those guys could make reading a phone book hilarious. Reading the cafeteria's hot lunch menu was always silly. Remembering "Meata-ballsa" still makes me smile. There were times our morning announcement banter might get us in trouble. Those days, after finishing, we'd quickly dash out of the PA room (making Three Stooges noises) before Principal Hagan could come out of his office and lecture us.

George's God

One morning, Doug Atkinson wanted to play a trick on George Barbehan, an outspoken atheist in his homeroom, so we made a plan. Doug started a religious debate with George in homeroom one morning (their homeroom was in a temporary building). Of course, we were listening over the PA. There weren't many people in the homeroom, so we could hear them very well. George was spouting off about the hydrogen atom nucleus.

As soon as George finished his main point, I spoke these words in a deep, booming, Charlton Heston voice: "Yes, George, there *is* a God!" According to Doug, George acted truly startled, grabbed his desk, and said something like, "That must be you, Alphonzo!" We never did figure out who 'Alphonzo' was.

Special Days

We did have a favorite trick. Most students were in their homerooms by the first warning bell, which was easy to confuse with the homeroom-starting bell. When we had a good friend whose birthday and homeroom number we knew, we'd turn on the PA in their room and in some of the adjacent rooms. After this first warning bell, we'd start announcing as if it were the normal time, saying, "Good morning, faculty and students. Please rise to sing Happy Birthday to _____." Then all three of us would sing in three-part harmony. To be fancy, before singing, we would hit the xylophone note corresponding to the first note of the song.

Chevy Chase

Usually, morning announcers are anonymous. However, during our banter we might have mentioned "Mikey, Jeffy, and Gordy" because one of the first things my Psychology teacher said to me was that my humor was like that of Chevy Chase. Not knowing who Chevy Chase was, I asked her what she meant. She said, "Your deadpan delivery." I only now realize that she must have been talking about our announcements.

Gene "the Bean," the infamous DJ

In that same Psychology class, I made friends with a junior, Gene Baxter. He was a zealous Elton John fan. He became a graduating senior and somehow joined our announcement team during the last couple months of the school year. All three of my fellow announcers were very tall (over 6' 3"), and all ended up in the radio business. Gene "the Bean" Baxter (6' 6") was the one to make national headlines.

The 'Bean' Coincidence

Much later, in the 1990's, my son Gavin made friends with Evan Waugh, the son of Bob Waugh, a famous DJ at WHFS, a progressive rock station. We were invited to the Waugh's for dinner. The subject of his being a DJ came up. I mentioned that the only DJ I knew was Gene Baxter, who was somewhere out west. Bob said, "Gene Baxter! He's a DJ at KORQ, our LA sister station."

As if that wasn't coincidence enough, as we were leaving, Bob said, "Gene and I trade tapes of our new playlist songs every week. Here's Gene's tape from last week. You can keep it." I enjoyed Gene's taste in music—more melodic and less overwhelmed by rhythm than our local music. Gene was able to garner national publicity for his station when he and his co-host "got into trouble with their station and the Los Angeles County Sheriff's Department by airing a fake murder confession." You can read the rest of Gene's story by Googling "Gene Baxter radio."

We Came to Compete

Anxiously awaiting the math meet, I dismissed the super graphics on the cafeteria wall, which hopefully proclaimed, "Duval High is Number 1." We'd arrived to prove them wrong yet again. The silence was broken by the sounds of running feet. A sweat-drenched, gaunt frame was trying to talk through heaving air. "Come . . . quickly—accident." It was Brian Antonio's voice. We jumped up and ran to him.

Brian told the rest of our team to run to the school's office to find a phone. Brian and I dashed out toward the parking lot, into the blinding Maryland sunlight, and hopped into my parent's light blue, '66 Ford station wagon.

What Robert's Cougar looked like to us when new

Windows cranked down, front vent windows swung open, before we knew it we were out of the lot and at the first intersection. As I began to turn to go right, Antonio pushed the steering wheel to go straight, saying, "No, we took the backroad shortcut, straight ahead." Luckily, we made it across the four lanes, against the light, without being hit.

Antonio mentioned "fire hydrant," "fire," and "Robert's Cougar." I thought back to how lucky Cheng had been to receive that shiny, royal-green, black-topped Cougar as a gift the previous summer. Low-mileage, too. It couldn't be a serious accident, could it?

Prelude: Back to the Beginning

To get to the after-school math meet, we had used three cars. As always, the seniors were driving while briefing the younger teammates on typical math-meet tricks. To get the devious math problems right, they'd have to remember that "i" is the square root of negative one, quadratic equations, and carpeting stairs word problems. Just when you thought you'd seen through a problem's tricks, another one would trip you up.

We were the first to arrive at the meet because Duval was the closest high school to our Bowie. Mrs. Hyde, the Math Meet founder, hadn't even distributed the evenly spaced #2 pencils that marked our seats on the many cafeteria tables. Like matrix coordinates, each team would have one teammate across the first "row" of seats; then, also facing forward, their teammates would be in a column of cafeteria table seats behind them.

Some newbies were playing "Lunar Landing" on my big, fancy TI SR-52, the first programmable calculator. Though Armstrong had guided the first moon landing some seven years before, we owed much of our superb education to the Space Race started by the '57 Sputnik launch. Of course, the rules dictated that all of our calculators were to remain holstered once the meet began.

With 25 minutes until game time, worry started spreading through the team. Anxiety multiplied because our teacher/sponsor, Miss Collins, "was probably not coming." Without her, we weren't allowed to compete. Someone said that she had been seen grading papers, adding, "Bet she's forgotten; we have to go back and get her!" I alone was pleading, "Wait and see—don't panic."

Before I knew it, Robert Cheng, Doug Atkinson, and Brian Antonio were dashing out to Cheng's Cougar, leaving the rest of us behind. In an age long before cell phones, we could only wait for them. We had no idea that we would soon be roused by the word *accident*.

The Scene

We raced toward the accident on the less-than-two-lane road with no shoulders, which dropped off to a forest floor on each side. The dark, enclosing woods ended ahead on the right side to reveal sunlight. "Slow down, we're getting close," said Antonio. As the road dropped below us, it veered slightly left. We could see that the airborne Cougar had kept going straight before landing and going slightly off the road. A gushing geyser of water shot up from a jagged pipe where a hydrant once stood. It was flooding the low field about three car lengths behind the Cougar's carcass.

We were so happy to see Cheng and Atkinson, unhurt, standing beside the road and clear of the smoking car. Doug directed us to park on the dirt lane on the right just before the scene. Cheng, in shock, couldn't look away, saying, "No, no, no!" as if wanting to awake from a nightmare.

Doug looked down at their pile of rescued notebooks and books, then looked at the Cougar's rear window. He saw his crumpled, burgundy letterman jacket on the back-window shelf. "Do you think I can save my jacket?" Doug's hard-earned status symbol for playing on the varsity soccer team put him among the highest regarded athletic defenders of Bowie; not just a nerd. (The more complimentary "geek" was yet to become popular.)

The car lay tilted, its left wheels almost reaching the road. Flames started to appear in the front. The front headlights were amazingly intact, but between them was a U-shaped indentation that extended all the way to the middle of the hood. The windshield was unbroken. There didn't seem to be room for an engine under the area remaining between the windshield and the indentation. Seeing it bottomed out in the mud, gas tank in the rear, I yelled, "Doug, you'd better be quick!"

Sending for Help

As Doug hurried to get his jacket, I rushed down the lane toward the nearest house, thinking, "No one knows where we are—I must find a telephone." Pounding on the door, I noticed the empty driveway: no one home. The neighbor's house had a windowed front door. Was that a car in the driveway? Running over and knocking at their door only woke a deep-throated dog. It looked to be on a backyard run as I peered through the house.

I was just pulling back my elbow to break the pane by the doorknob when I heard the sound of a big pick-up pulling in the driveway. As I turned toward the mud-covered truck, the driver stepped out, his right hand still reaching into the truck. As I moved closer, he pointed to the black CB mike in his right palm, calmly saying, "I called it in. Anybody hurt?"

As we all gathered by the site, we could see the front tires sending up clouds of black smoke. If only we could direct the water toward the car or drag the car back on top of the jagged water pipe . . . but it was dug in too hard and too far away. And the fire traveled quickly, flames shooting out the windows, black coupe top curling and peeling off the hot roof. Soon the rear tires caught and we moved even farther away.

Senseless

Antonio said, "Help is on the way. No reason for you to just wait here. I am only on the B team this week. I can stay while you go back to Duval." Arms around Cheng, Doug and I got into the station wagon and left. On the way back, we tried to comfort him despite his "what ifs": what if the long straightaway hadn't dropped and bent to the left; what if the hydrant hadn't been there; what if he just hadn't driven today. . . .

The incredible irony of the scene was overwhelming: the shooting column of brightly-lit water in front of the dense, slowly billowing clouds of blackest smoke. Cheng added that it was also ironic that he was driving without his glasses at first and Doug and Brian helped him put them on long before the accident. At Duval, everyone surrounded us with questions, including Miss Collins. The worry about her presence was all for nothing.

We were all in shock. At the suggestion that Cheng and Atkinson, two of our best A team members, sit it out, Cheng said, "Are you kidding? We came to compete!" And compete they did: getting every problem correct and catching some of the tricks in the team problem. Bowie's A Math Team would capture the County title again that year. Cheng and I were even chosen for the Washington, DC, regional team that competed up in Hartford, Connecticut.

Robert and me

Worthy of a story in the local paper? Nah, not even a mention. Most of the school was unaware of their scholar-letes. The highly competitive math-meet structure created camaraderie that motivated us to teach each other. This incident deeply impressed upon me (and others) the need to forcibly say "no" and calm worry frenzies that could spiral out of control into needless actions.

Action Cheng

Robert was a devoted audiophile. He invited us over to listen as he played the Beatles' White Album backwards when it was all the rage. The distorted voice hinted, "Paul is dead," and he'd ask, "Hear that? What does that mean?" We'd discuss all the possibilities.

My parents bought a stereo system that happened to be capable of quadraphonic sound. Robert knew the best song to demonstrate its capabilities. A few of us would often stand by the speakers that were sitting on the living room bookshelf to listen to the instrumental, "Frankenstein," by the Edgar Winter Group. The descending helicopter sound slowly wound around us, causing us to smile in amazement.

Robert and his two-years-younger brother would listen to records while doing homework in their bedroom. By 11th grade, their record collection was so huge that he needed to find a way to listen to each side of every long-playing record in a random order. In our computer class, we learned about the "random number generator" function. Robert quickly put it to practical use. Using our crude school computer, he developed a database and program that printed out a randomized list of each side of all his records.

When we did our math homework together at his house, Robert's youngest brother would always be watching *Star Trek* (there was only one back then). We'd take breaks by playing ping-pong. Robert showed me how to hold the paddle "Chinese style." By holding it like a pen, it makes your moves much mightier than when holding it like a sword.

In math class we learned how to use Gaussian elimination. Robert invented a different way to get the same results and called it "Cheng elimination." During that year's class, it was important to remember that the correct order of notation is (row, column) not (column, row). Just knowing "R"obert "C"heng made it easy to keep that order in mind.

Where Am I? What Happened?

One day we came too close to an actual Cheng elimination. It was a yearly tradition for a bunch of us teenage Kenilworth kids to get together to play football on the field behind our old elementary school on the day after Thanksgiving. The field was as hard as concrete. We must have been playing tackle because there was often a broken bone.

During one of these games, Robert was thrown hard to the ground and landed on his head with a horrible thud. We rushed over to his seemingly lifeless body. It seemed like an eternity before he revived. He had the bewildered look of waking from a dream with no idea of where he was.

Days later, when Robert told us the doctor's diagnosis, it was the first time I had heard the word "hematoma." He explained it simply as "a bruise on the brain and a pocket of fluid between my brain and my skull." Yuck!

Bully on Our Bus

There was a nasty bully who rode our school bus to high school. Unfortunately, he lived at the very end of my street. Every other year he would get bolder and bolder in extending his terrorizing upward on Kemper Lane until I fought with him and put him back in his place.

In his vulgar and unrepeatable language, he often boasted that his father had fought in the Korean War and that he hated anyone who was "Oriental." Sometimes, on the bus ride home, I would notice this bully yelling at Robert and threatening to hit him as he stood over him. Robert's passive response did nothing to deter the bully. I would just push him aside and sit next to Robert.

Wendy's

Whenever I eat a Wendy's burger, I'm reminded of Robert. He introduced me to them. We were sitting on the left side of a bus on the way to Hartford, Connecticut, to compete in a regional math meet competition. We had been chosen for the Washington, DC, area team of 22 students. As the bus pulled  over so we could get lunch, Robert said, "Good, a Wendy's!"

Looking at the red sign, I thought it strange to have a little girl 's picture and her first name, so I asked Robert about it. He replied, "You never heard of Wendy's? They have the best hamburgers!" My family didn't go out to eat much. To me nothing was as good as Mom's home-cooked meals. Much later I discovered that Wendy was the founder's daughter.

The hamburgers were delicious there, reminding me of long before, when Mom and Dad took my brother and me to McDonald's for the first time. Its huge yellow arch structures were futuristically fantastic, and its commercials at the time boasted, "Feed a family of four for less than a dollar," which is inconceivable now.

The winners of the big math meet were a few teams from New York City. That afternoon, Robert led me on an adventure. He said, "Let's walk to a bar and drink some beer." When I argued that we were under age and would get caught, he countered, "Not if we act normal." So, we went into the dark bar, sat at a round café table, and ordered our beer. Once it arrived, I relaxed as we chatted and enjoyed our beers.

Juipo

Robert's Chinese heritage intrigued me. Naturally I asked him about common Chinese words. He said that the word he most often heard from his father was during family shopping outings when they asked for things. It was pronounced "swan la," which means "forget it." However, he was more reluctant to tell me his middle name.

With the help of his mother, I learned that his middle name was spelled "Juipo." This sent me on a scramble to the library to learn what it meant and how to pronounce it. Despite my difficulty learning French, I had been trying to learn some Russian during my bike rides to the library, so I knew where the language books were. I had only gotten as far as temporarily memorizing the Russian alphabet. Learning a language from only a book is like learning to pole-vault from a telephone conversation.

The Chinese translation books proved even more daunting than Russian ones. Each syllable has a totally different meaning depending on the inflection when spoken. After looking in several huge books, I had about a dozen possibilities. All were wrong—especially the ones pertaining to farmyard animals.

Finally, Robert allowed his mother to tell me about his middle name. The pronunciation of "Juipo" is somewhat similar to "Robert" in Chinese, but more important, it means "One who will become great through use of his mind." This was such a wonderful prediction, especially given Robert's success today. I hoped that some of this might rub off on me, since I had been baptized "Robert" by a stubborn priest who wouldn't admit that "Gordon" was a saint's name.

Taking the "High" Road

In high school some teenagers were trying cigarettes and marijuana. Addiction ruined many bright futures. I was afraid that some of Robert's friends might send him down the wrong path. This inspired me to write a poem to him to convince him to aim for the long-range natural high. Purposely, it avoided all the typical clichés and even the word "drug."

This poem was the first thing Rob mentioned to me when I started writing these "Cheng Stories." Although lost now and amateurish, it was heartening to discover that my fumbling words meant something to someone. You might never know how much your love has helped others. Whatever love you have received, you must reradiate it tenfold, even a hundredfold, in the hopes of brightening others.

Our Paths Separate

Proximity is a big part of a close friendship. During the summer after high school, I became busy working downtown as an intern with the DOT/Federal Railroad Administration and working on my VW. This left less time to hang out with Robert. Then we went to different universities and lost touch with each other.

During high school, everyone was fairly quiet about their college plans. Robert had told me long ago that when he was born, a large sum of money had been invested for his future college, so I knew he'd be going to an expensive private school. I was led to schools that could help me become a professional architect most efficiently.

Years later I was working as an architect at CRSS a few blocks from the White House. My other responsibility was computer system manager. My reward for streamlining the functioning of the office's PCs, Macintoshes, and Linux CADD workstations was getting back to architecture work. One day I noticed an editorial in the monthly magazine from our PC supplier, Gateway. It mentioned a few things that sounded familiar, including the Baltimore Orioles. Because the author's name was Rob, I took a chance and sent an email to Gateway Computers in Iowa. Happily, it worked, and Robert and I were reconnected.

Teacher Vignettes

My first 10th-grade class was Mrs. D'Michalis's Western Civilization. I was surprised that most of my classmates were 11th and 12th graders. The lessons fascinated me. Before this class I didn't even know the relationship between the Greek, Egyptian, and Roman Empires. Why hadn't this been taught way back in elementary school?

There was an oafish bully sitting near me who pestered the girls. I felt like punching him to make him stop. Then, on a daily basis, he started cussing back and forth with this little pinheaded black guy. Finally, they started boasting about how big their gangs were. This grew into a planned gang rumble after school. I worried that Tasker Junior High violence was here, too. Getting on the bus that afternoon I saw their "gang" fight. It was only the oaf and the pinhead hurling insults at each other.

*

In 10th grade, our biology classes were not separated by ability, so Mr. Padar had to teach at the level of the slowest students. Despite the slow pace, I stayed respectful and attentive. One day after class, he showed me a cardboard computer kit that taught basic I/O, bits, bytes, hexidecimal, etc. Unbelievably, he gave it to me. I was very thankful.

*

The summer before 10th grade, I rode my bike to Drivers Ed class at Bowie High. Our big group watched movies narrated by Walter Cronkite. Some of them showed statistics about teenage driver fatalities, but more impressive were all the gruesome crash recreations.

After classroom lectures, they would take one class at a time into the room of "modern" driving simulators. They didn't have a bell that rang every time you ran someone over, as classmate Mark Ciomei had told us. In fact, on the first day I was still buckling my seat belt and trying to shift out of park when I looked up and saw the class's movie showing a view of us driving down the street as the narrator was talking us through a turn.

The actual driving in a car was much better—partly because this was my first taste of meeting kids from the other two junior highs that fed into Bowie Senior High. The two who took turns driving with me were lanky Chris Cressy and sweet country-gal Lee Anne Reiter. Our instructor was a young guy who was very calm and cool.

One time he wanted us to stop in at Hardee's (where Taco Bell now stands) so he could buy a drink. We all cranked down the windows and climbed out of them like the "Dukes of Hazzard." Speaking of hazard, one time I was driving in front of the Glenn Dale fire station when obstacles popped out like in a simulator movie. Even though I was going 40, a huge truck was tailgating me—a typical harassment of student drivers. Then a fire truck pulled out into my lane, so I swerved into the incoming lane to pass it. To avoid the oncoming school bus, I floored it to get back in my lane.

As I straightened out and stopped for the train-crossing crossbar coming down, I barely missed the woman and baby carriage stepping off the corner. These few seconds must have flustered the teacher sitting next to me, but all he said was, "Yeah, shoot the gap, good, shoot the gap." In my mirror I noticed that the two back-seat kids looked shocked.

*

Mrs. Kassabian's 11th grade English class was always full of laughs. She truly loved us and adored even her students from earlier classes. While waiting for the class bell to ring, she'd often look out of her classroom door at the passing students and say something like, "Oh, there's my little Randy!" She'd be in the hall like a flash, looking up at him while pinching his cheek like a visiting aunt.

When it was time to get down to business, she would say, "OK, enough fun, this is serious stuff." Sometimes we took turns reading aloud passages from our classroom textbooks and then analyzing them. One day the text was from a sailing novel, probably by Joseph Conrad or Herman Melville.

Kelly Meyer

This day it was Kelly Meyer's turn to read. Kelly looked far more mature than most high school girls and would always act in a suggestive way, but her quick wit revealed her underlying intelligence. Once you got to know her, you discovered that "she was just drawn that way." So, Mrs. Kassabian said, "Kelly, could you start reading at the top of page 261?"

After Kelly read the chapter title, "The Wayfaring Seamen," she made an expression that told us what she was really thinking. Then it went on about the quarterdeck and a seaman saved from the sea's deadly grip. Every word was given a second meaning that made it hard for us to suppress our laughter.

"The poor wretch was so thankful to be aboard and feel the poop under his feet." Here she quickly ad-libbed, "I bet it felt good between his toes." The whole room broke down laughing.

*

Mr. Long's Computer Math class was a great opportunity, unlike the "Data Processing" classes that simply taught how to punch IBM cards. We learned to create formulas and write simple computer programs to see how they work on a real computer.

There weren't computer screens back then. We went into a closet to type on a "line printer," a big electric typewriter on a stand that loudly printed what we typed on wide sheets of perforated computer paper. Our programs could be saved on perforated rolls of ticker-tape paper that we kept rolled up in old plastic camera-film canisters.

Here's an example of a theoretical problem Mr. Long asked us to solve with him on the blackboard. A dog tied to a stake goes to three random points at the limit of his leash. What is the average area of all possible random triangles that could be formed in this way? Mr. Long started finding random points on the circle by generating random values along the x-axis on the blackboard, but I pointed out that only by using polar coordinates would they be truly random.

*

To practice our French, a friend and I would try vainly to communicate only in French during outings. The week before 11th grade started, I had my first dream in French. It was a movie about a queen. I could understand it without subtitles. When the closing credits started to scroll, one name stood out: "Robert Amoruso." As soon as I awoke, I told Mom about this dream and the name.

Imagine my surprise when on the first day of French II class Madame Huff called attendance and said, "Robert Amoruso." He was a year older and someone I'd never seen. We ended up doing group projects together such as making beef bourguignon at his house and putting on a *Six Million Dollar Man* skit in French for the class.

*

Ms. Meador's 12th grade AP English class did more than give us an awareness of bird imagery and punctuation and prepare us for the Advanced Placement test. She also graded on "varying sentence length." Then there's the lighter side. In her other AP class, the ever-unpredictable Brian McLean performed a pantyhose commercial with shaved legs.

She promised that if anyone got a 5, the highest rating, on the English AP test she would raise their class grade to an A. This was important to me because my English grade for each quarter was A, A, A, then B. In the crazy school system this meant my grade for the year was . . . B. Only Matt Westbrook and I scored 5 on the AP test. By the time she found out my test score, it was too late to change my B. No big deal now. Queen Anne's 100-point grading system was much better and more straightforward in my eyes.

Physics was as fun for me as "advanced kindergarten." You rolled around carts to understand forces. We watched water ripple on water tables to explore how light waves travel. One time Mr. Dotson asked a big soccer player, Rusty Curtis, to sit on a revolving stool in front of class with weights in his hands. As he brought the weights in, his slow turning became a rapid revolution, like an ice skater. It was all due to "conservation of angular momentum."

One day I came to class and Mr. Dotson had two big boxes of sand hanging from a stick. When he moved a third sandbox close to one of them, it swung closer because it was attracted by gravity! He also helped Doug Atkinson and me study for the AP Physics test. We wanted to go beyond the other four AP courses offered at Bowie High.

Other Memorable Classes

One of my favorite teachers was Mr. Haworth, famous for his AP U.S. History class. His daily slide shows and interesting narrative made the info memorable. The weekly in-class essays were scary, but prepared us well. I took his class in 11th grade. It was there I met classmate Karen Cook, who was in 12th grade.

*

Only one year of Physical Education was required. While we were playing flag football in 10th grade PE, I was distracted by the distant girls' class practicing archery. This cost me a hit in the chin by a blocker's sharp elbow. After I was sent to the infirmary, Mom brought me to the doctor to get it stitched closed.

*

In Mr. Dove's Photography class, we made pinhole cameras and developed our film in his big darkroom with its light-lock revolving door. We even used the enlarging stand to create neat double-exposure special effects.

*

My Drafting and House Design teacher, Mr. Rodney Reed, had a retro flattop haircut. We listened to a top-40 station while we drafted. Meanwhile, the Ford and Chevy "gearhead" factions would trash-talk each other.

*

After Calculus class, Robert Cheng and I would dare each other to go up to girls we adored and compliment them in the hall. This resulted in some comic situations on the breezeway bridge.

*

In Art class I was upset when my detailed drawing of the Statue of Liberty was stolen from my cubbyhole. After that I began finishing my projects quickly. The teacher would let me go across the hall to sit in on the very informative Independent Living class. The perky Home Ec teacher taught everything from setting up a household economy to choosing cuts of beef. Years later, I would often buy the London Broil that she recommended as economical yet tasty.

It's Academic

A few of us juniors were curious to see what our seniors were doing for the It's Academic team. We were friends with the book-smart senior core primarily through the Math team. They were mostly quiet and shy. All of them would go on to highly prestigious universities. One of them, Marcus, was an average athlete who would relax with us by shooting hoops. During a college break, he said that he was surprised when MIT promoted him to their "jock dorm."

This senior group was having a summer meeting to practice for It's Academic in a house in the Somerset section. Curious to see how they practiced, I went that night. Naturally, it began with socializing by standing in small conversations. The group dynamics were interesting to watch. The practicing never started, though. It turned into an excuse for a geek (or "nerd" back then) party.

There was one loud character who often bragged that studying was for dummies, and geniuses were naturally smart. The quieter geeks who thought it would be better to practice didn't have a chance to speak. The team that year had the disadvantage of having their match scheduled early in the school year. Although extremely intelligent, like many Bowie It's Academic teams, they were eliminated in the first round.

Next Year

By nature I'm not very good at audio learning or quickly replying. During lectures, the only way I could make the information stick was to simultaneously scribble down notes. This way, lecture material was fixed in my graphic memory. I seldom looked at the notes later. Therefore, when I was elected as It's Academic club president in my senior year, I thought my chances of making the team were doubtful.

It was an old habit to allow only seniors on the three-person team. However, some show questions came from

1977 sponsors Mr. Long and Miss Twomey

subjects we had studied years ago. I convinced the club members that we should allow every student in the school to try out. We might find some ringers. Through school-wide announcements, we soon had some sophomores and juniors attending our open lunch practice sessions—including a couple of ringers.

We practiced in Mr. Long's computer math classroom during most open lunch hours. Fortunately, previous clubs had written down questions and answers from old It's Academic shows on index cards. The beautiful Miss Twomey, one of our club sponsors, showed us shoeboxes full of these cards. During our practices she peppered us with questions. We mimed pushing buzzers while making a buzzing sound before being called on to answer. One club member, Ron Natalie, was good at imitating the show host, Mac McGarry, when taking turns quizzing us.

We shared maps of state capitals, historic timelines, periodic tables, and lists of presidents to study and memorize. The pop culture that has crept into today's *Jeopardy* was not on the show. To answer our curiosity, we did not have Wikipedia in our pockets. Most houses had

a set of encyclopedias. Our *World Book Encyclopedia* at home had about 20 volumes plus 10 "Year Books" with updates. They took up a whole shelf.

Selecting the Bowie Team

When it got closer to the date of our show, we held team tryouts that were scored. Each of us had a small "tap bell" that we'd use to ring in. Somehow I scored the highest, so I became team captain. Dennis Fitzgerald, a junior, and Stephen Uehling, a sophomore, also earned team membership.

Gordon Cook, Robert Cheng, and Doug Atkinson

Dennis and Stephen had an impressive knowledge of things I'd never even heard about. More importantly, I knew which were their areas of expertise. We built more than teamwork by practicing together; we could read each other's minds. Our whole club contributed much uncredited support, especially our alternative team members, Gordon Cook, Robert Cheng, and Doug Atkinson.

Game Day

We had asked our cheerleaders if they would join us on the TV show. Before each commercial break, each team's cheerleaders would be featured. Ours weren't interested.

The two local It's Academic leagues, Washington and Baltimore, were each composed of 81 teams. Somehow, Bowie was usually assigned to the Baltimore League. There also were a few Montgomery County teams in our league.

Sadly, just before our first appearance the rest of my family had to fly to upstate New York for my grandfather's funeral. As I was riding up to Baltimore's Television Hill in my teacher's car that December, any of my nervousness was driven out by sorrow. We must make the most of our time.

On the Baltimore TV channels, you often heard, "Coming to you from Television Hill!" It was a surprise to see that the station was actually a tiny brick building perched atop a small peak. TV studios look much bigger and sturdier on the screen at home. I first noticed an odd single-lane bowling alley closely flanked by wavy blackout curtains.

The three sections of the audience bleachers formed a slightly cupped shape. From our seats we could easily see the crowd across the flat-black floor. When the bright lights came on and the big TV cameras moved into position, the audience faded from view. All eyes focused on our affable host, Mac McGarry, standing behind his podium. He and his distinctive voice were an institution.

As he read each question from a card in his hand, all competitors on the three teams listened intently to every word. Often I rang our buzzer early during the "Grab Bag" rounds, then looked to the teammate who had that expertise. Even though "Mac" stopped reading as soon as I buzzed in, I was confident in my teammates' knowledge. That was another benefit of all that practice.

The show ended with our score at 500 to Polytechnic's 440 and John Carroll's 270. We were so happy and relieved to somehow win our first match. That was the only thing we had worked toward. Then it hit us; we'd be coming back for another match. We were just happy that we

Dennis Fitzgerald, me, and Stephen Uehling

had moved up from just one of the 81 teams to be among the top 27 in the single-elimination contest.

Second Match

I wasn't very nervous during our second match because we had already done better than most Bowie teams. Anything else was just icing on the cake. Our three alternative members gave us much-needed moral support and helped psyche out the other teams. By using our same fast-buzzer-teamwork methods, we won yet again. This put us into the top nine teams in the Baltimore area. Too bad we couldn't officially claim a "County Champs" title like our football team had done that year.

My parents and siblings were able to attend these matches. One match must have been on St. Patrick's Day because my little brother Colin was caught wearing a big shamrock during some of the crowd shots. The matches aired on TV weeks after filming.

Third Match

For our third match, our team was sitting at a slightly elevated console in the middle. Despite how they look on TV, these consoles are fairly rickety. Stephen Uehling noticed ripples in his plastic water glass. In movies this is the sign of a coming earthquake. He asked me, "What is that?" I pointed down to my knee rapidly vibrating up and down. It was an uncontrollable outlet for my nervousness due to the rarefied air of advancing so far. We did well, but not well enough to win.

Aftermath

Before our matches, winning an It's Academic scholarship was not even mentioned. During a game, the scores didn't sidetrack us. Any such distractions were ignored. Winning one match was our only focus. No one was counting their chickens before they hatched.

However, since we had exceeded our expectations, we did win scholarship money. We assumed it would be divided among our team.

It was surprising to learn that the scholarship money would be going to seniors in our school who were selected by an independent group of teachers. Announcements went out to ask those interested to submit essays. The scholarship money was eventually given equally to Donna Scalise, Teri Vossler, and myself.

We had advanced farther than any Bowie It's Academic team had before or since (as of 2017). The county finished construction of a windowless "magnet" high school in nearby Greenbelt in 1976. This magnet, Eleanor Roosevelt High School, would start pulling away many Bowie scholars, including my youngest brother Colin and, many years later, my daughter Lauriane.

*

From the *It's Academic* official website:

The *Guinness Book of World Records* has recognized *It's Academic* as the world's longest-running TV quiz show. Started in 1961 on NBC4 in Washington D.C., the program continues as America's foremost high school quiz show. The school year 2015-2016 [was] our 55th season of telecasts.

Maurice James "Mac" McGarry hosted the Washington-area *It's Academic* for half a century, from our first telecast in 1961 until his retirement in 2011. He was also quizmaster for the Baltimore area *It's Academic* for 34 years.

In addition to the current programs in Washington, DC, Baltimore, Central Virginia, and Hawaii, *It's Academic* is produced under other names in Cleveland (*Academic Challenge*) and Pittsburgh (*Hometown High-Q*). In the past, it has also been produced in Chicago, New York, Los Angeles, Philadelphia, Buffalo, Cincinnati, Denver, Boston, Jacksonville, San Diego, Norfolk, Phoenix and Raleigh.

More Than a Gold Tassel

Traditionally, the National Honor Society (NHS) was only an honorary title that boosted your qualifications when you applied for acceptance at a university. There were four requirements for NHS: grade point average of 3.0 on a 4.0 scale, volunteer aid, leadership, and character. Because it took time to gain the necessary experience, only 11th graders could apply at Bowie. Those accepted were invited to an induction ceremony near the end of their junior year; therefore, the NHS usually only had time to organize one event such as a car wash to raise a small amount for charity. At graduation, there was an asterisk next to each member's name, and they wore a gold tassel on their mortarboard (that big flat hat).

NATIONAL HONOR SOCIETY

st row: Sharon Frink, Peggy Pesce, Sarah Stanely, Adie Solomon (treasurer), Kris Johnson (secretary), Gordon Stewart (president), Sharon ppel (vice-president), Lynne Bremer, Stephanie Brown, Mary Mead. 2nd row: Lori Long, Anne Landis, Jennifer Dougherty, Lori Mihok, Betsy ickels, Carla Becker, Teri Vossler, Gretchen Yost, Deborah Fajer, Gordon Cook, Mike Moran, Sharon Samuels. 3rd row: Dorothy McIntyre, my Fisher, Doug Atkinson, Robert Chen, Allen Brisentine, Harry Wannemacher, Michele Sison, Joe Faber, Matt Westbrook, Sue McCullen, elinda Miles, Debbie Atwood.

At the beginning of our senior year I was elected president (no one else really wanted the job). Immediately I searched the NHS file drawer and found an announcement for NHS scholarships scrunched up in the back of the cabinet. The deadline for essay applications was in two weeks! We quickly got the word out, especially through my morning announcements. Among those who applied, three of us received NHS scholarships.

Visibility

We wanted more people to be aware of NHS. At the time, car rallies were popular on many TV shows such as *Hart to Hart* and *McMillan and Wife*. We knew nothing about them but decided to hold one anyway and make it more of a treasure hunt.

To determine the route and find interesting clues, we drove around Bowie looking for curious things and thinking up clever tricks. On these afternoons while riding around with five witty and pretty girls, I felt very lucky. It seemed much better than "spending the night getting drunk with a carful of girls at Whitemarsh Park," as a guy I knew would boast.

The Social Scene Sidebar

People often complained that there was nothing for teenagers to do in Bowie. Many kids would get drunk or high at the Hilltop Plaza parking lot, or at Whitemarsh Park, a secluded big cul-de-sac of ball fields. One of their wise parents would plead, "If you hang out with the owls at night, you can't soar with the eagles during the day."

On the other hand, most of my friends found many more beneficial enjoyments. There were house dance parties, bowling, trips to the beach in Ocean City, school dances, and movies (though Bowie's only theater only had old movies). One of my favorite activities was to go roller skating up in Crofton.

From a guy's point of view, dating was usually calling a girl (or girls) on Wednesday night to set dates for that Friday and/or Saturday.

Gentlemen don't kiss and tell, and I'm sticking to that here. Those who talk big, kiss little. I didn't spend much time tying up the house phone. Infrequently, I'd write letters to pen pals or distant friends.

One time we were out on a "triple date" in Doug's three-row VW bus. He drove us to the train crossing on Old Fletchertown Road, where the road slopes up like a ski ramp. As the bus flew over the tracks, my date and I, in the rear seat, were thrown against the ceiling. Whenever someone spotted a one-headlight car, they'd yell, "Pid-dinkle!" If a guy said it first, he was kissed by his date. However, if the girl was first, she could slap or kiss him.

Back to the NHS Rally

After we had created directions for a clue-filled route, we typed them up and ran mimeographed copies (dittos). Every so often our puzzles included a "street-name clue" to help cars get back on track when lost. We charged a small entrance fee of five dollars. The total collected was divided among the top three winners.

I (in my Redskins jacket) sign in an entrant.

On the morning of rally day, a Saturday, we had several dozen participants signed up in two-person teams. To spread the NHS name, each vehicle was given a big red tag with "NHS car rally" written in large letters that had to be displayed in its windshield.

While one car rally organizer was signing in the latecomers, I took a copy of our instructions and drove off to make a quick check of the route. It was 15 minutes before our staggered start was scheduled to begin. I told one of my assistants to delay the start until I returned with the corrections. She was handing out the red windshield tags to those arriving in the high school entry circle.

The first clue was to turn right after the eighth metrobus stop sign on Belair Drive, but I couldn't believe that seven of the eight had been knocked down! I raced around checking more clues and noting changes on my copy. Finally, I decided it was time to head back to tell everyone these corrections.

Returning to Belair Drive by Spindle Lane, I was shocked to see a car with a red NHS rally tag coming toward me on Kenhill Drive. They must have started early and were now lost! Another lost soul was slowly driving up Belair Drive from my right looking for clues, and a third rally car came down Belair Drive from my left. They pulled over when they recognized my red VW bug. The staggered start must have been releasing cars without waiting at all!

As the three cars tried to flag me down, I knew I had to avoid any contact that would give them an unfair advantage, so I took off back to the school. There I discovered that my assistant had been convinced by the impatient entrants to start before I returned. What a mess!

Janice Pritchard gazes out beside team driver Linda Salisbury.

There was no way to contact anyone. We hoped the street-name clues would get them back on course. Communication by cell phones was 30 years in the future, and students' cars weren't equipped with the expensive Citizens Band radios from the CB craze of the early 70s. Though we'd timed the course to take 1½ hours, the fastest finisher took 2½ hours. Our finish-line group had to wait hours for the last arrivals at the secret end location.

Surprisingly, the entrants weren't furious, but rather enjoyed our tricky puzzles. Maybe by starting early they had taken responsibility for any problems. The winners were the team of Donna Scalise and Mike Collins, childhood sweethearts since ninth grade. I knew both of them well, but separately. At fifth-grade recess, Mike and I played the tag game our class invented, "Sacrifice."

Mike Collins and Donna Scalise (not visible) at the rally in their van

After high school we lost touch. In 2016, my daughter-in-law, Larissa, asked if I knew the parents of one of her best friends, Liliana Collins. We both agreed that her parents, Mike and Donna, are two of the nicest, most wonderful, most beautiful people.

Our Last NHS Duty

As we started planning the induction ceremony for the next year's Honor students, I realized why no one wanted my job. The outgoing president had to give a speech at the ceremony. Fortunately, a free but very effective Toastmasters public speaking class a few years before had prepared me for this, but when the new mayor of Bowie, Audrey Scott, accepted our guest speaker invitation, I knew my speech would pale in comparison.

Speaking of pale, I was still recovering from the mononucleosis caught from a soccer team water jug. For inspiration, I copied quotes from a Bartlett's quote book in the library. My mistake was incorporating too many of them into my speech.

Bowie mayor Audrey Scott

Later, Audrey was elected to a seat on the County Council. Then, two decades after speaking at this ceremony in the high school cafeteria, she was one of the politicians who helped BRAVA, the nonprofit I founded in 1995, build a performance center connected to the high school. Afterwards, Audrey was appointed to a position at the state level.

Enshrining the Past

Months before my Bowie graduation, I received an invitation to another school's commencement ceremony. It was similar to the invitations I had mailed out. After opening the fancy envelope and seeing the Saturday date, I immediately found the return envelope under the fancy tissue paper and checked "Yes" on the RSVP card. My reasons for going:

1. It was from my long-lost best friend from elementary school, Brian Goobeck. He was graduating from Archbishop Carroll, a Catholic boys school in northeast DC. I had heard about it when one of my younger neighborhood friends, John Dagirmanjian, went there.

2. The graduation was being held at the Shrine of the Immaculate Conception, which sounded much more magical than the location of Bowie's graduation on a basketball court in the University of Maryland's Cole Field House. For some reason, I thought a shrine was something shiny on a hill. The "shine/shrine" connection was just another one of my strange visual word associations. Since the ceremony was being held "at" and not "in," I figured it must be happening outdoors.

3. The guest speaker was to be Alex Haley, author of the recent blockbuster novel *Roots*, about the generations of his ancestors back to "Kunte Kinte," who had been captured in Africa and sold as a slave in Maryland. That January we'd all watched the many-part TV miniseries that was based on his book. It broke previous TV viewing records and won nine Emmy awards.

Being There

I thought this shrine, like all the important sites in DC, must be located around the Mall, Washington's monumental core. Looking over the map the night before, I discovered that it was located closer to Bowie, as the crow flies. Our big Route 50, which runs through Bowie, quickly brings us to the heart of DC, so I didn't allow time for all the side streets and stop lights. My drive also took longer because I was driving stick shift while dealing with a folded paper map and watching for signs.

The "Catholic University" sign meant I was almost there. I wondered, "Is there a university for each religion?" Then a giant white stone church appeared, illuminated

by the sunshine. The Shrine looked like an unornamented modern version of those ancient European cathedrals. I parked close by. After straightening my tie in the mirror, I got out and put on my coat. The air was mercifully cool, but the mountain of steps was strangely empty. Was I too late?

At the top of the stairs I pulled up my wristwatch sleeve to see that I still had a couple minutes, but maybe I had the wrong date? Inside I sought reassurance from a stack of programs. On the page of names, I found "Brian Goobeck." Below it another name, "Leo Green Jr," caught my eye. Way back during one of our kindergarten recesses, Leo was the one in our circle of stick-rubbing little Indians who came closest to making fire.

Inside the dark cavernous structure, I proceeded down the central aisle toward the source of light. It was a distant shimmering ceiling covered in shiny gold. Because my eyes were still adjusting to the darkness, I could barely see that the pews on both sides were totally full. Sadly, I came to realize that I'd have to find a seat far in the back, so I turned around and started to walk back.

A familiar friendly voice loudly whispered, "Gordon! Come here, we'll make room." It was the Honorable Leo Green, Senior, young Leo's father. As a State Senator, the previous year he had invited Joey Faber, me, and our families to the State Senate, where he presented a special bill. Joey and I had the highest PSAT scores in our grade at Bowie High, and the bill was to honor us. (Joey is the one I had a scuffle with in third grade. Eighteen years after this graduation, Senator Green would be the prime mover in starting and funding the construction of the Bowie Center for the Performing Arts.)

After clambering over and into the pew, I found myself among the Greens' six younger children. One of them sat on my knees to make room. Knowing that the speaker was probably going to talk about his genealogical research, my mind wandered to my own ancestors. It was the perfect place to ponder about the many relatives on both sides of my tree.

Mom had mentioned her family's stories: the ancient Latvian concertmaster violinists, the three McAdoo siblings who changed religion and were disinherited, and other stories. Dad had told of his adventures and how his father, Abner (1891–1976), had taught himself about the new field of electricity rather than follow the outdated path of staying on the family horse farm. This skill enabled him to support his family and others through the Great Depression. We also had a connection to Mary Stuart, Queen of Scots (and France for a time). Both my parents had given me an inner confidence with this knowledge of my athletic, intelligent, and musical ancestors. Fortunately, an opportunity led to my first foray into genealogy.

Why I Made a Stewart Descendants Tree

I had found the tempting puzzle a few years earlier. We happened to be in my dad's West Carthage hometown when our Stewart branch was gathering in nearby Whetstone Gulf (in upstate New York, a "gulf" is a narrow valley cut by a stream). At this reunion in 1974 or 75, everyone gathered around a series of picnic tables along the stream to chat and eat during the day.

It was a large group because Dad and his father each had eight siblings. Among the hundred or so people, there was a large group that kept apart from the rest. I was told that they were the Patchens. Most people, especially the young, didn't know how we were connected. Later, in Grandpa's house, we looked through old family Bibles to see the births that had been recorded. A small diagram gave me the names of the children of our most distant Stewart ancestor that was known at the time, James Stewart, a Vermont native (1772-1835).

I wanted to practice my architectural lettering on something worthwhile, and writing down the descendants in this family tree was a perfect project. Dad was able to bring a huge sheet of Mylar graph paper home from work. Most family trees were arranged vertically, but with 100 people in the current generation, it was better to progress horizontally, descending from James on the left.

STEWART

DRAWN BY Gordon Mead Stewart

August 1976

At the Stewart reunion in 1976, the huge tree was a big hit. Many people came over and wrote in missing and new information on the print. Even the Patchens came over. A few days later, my cousin Bruce and I visited many cemetery office records and headstones to fill in the missing info. Despite all

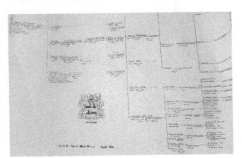

these descendants from our James Stewart, only my two brothers and I were left to carry on the name.

Back to Reality

Of course, when the famous Alex Haley was introduced during the graduation ceremony, my daydreaming stopped as I focused on his words. Surprisingly, he didn't concentrate on the evils of slavery, but instead his baritone voice gave a more universal message about all of us finding our roots. It encouraged me to go beyond my initial search. Since I wasn't compulsively taking notes as usual, I couldn't engrave his words into my visually oriented mind, but here are some words from his other speeches:

"In every conceivable manner, the family is (our) link to our past, bridge to our future."

"We all come from some family with a native heritage . . . know that you can build on their foundation . . . bits and pieces of a patchwork of family history . . . maintain family continuity."

"We are becoming too much of a youth-oriented society; we are suffering from a lack of rootedness."

"Take pride in the qualities of your ancestors. Take the stories from older people in your family to heart, because once they pass away, everything is lost."

Afterwards, Mr. Haley was kind enough to take time to see us individually. When my turn came, as he signed my program, I mentioned the family tree that I had created. Then we shook hands. He was the first nationally famous person I'd ever met.

*

From Wiki:

Haley has stated that the most emotional moment of his life occurred on September 29, 1967, when he stood at the site in Annapolis, Maryland, where his ancestor had arrived from Africa in chains exactly 200 years before. A memorial depicting Haley reading a story to young children gathered at his feet has since been erected in the center of Annapolis.

Saved for Last

1. Were you eager to be allowed to drive a car?

Definitely! You get to an age where the freedom of movement of your bicycle is not enough. Although my and other parents willingly drove us everywhere, I looked forward to exploring on a whim. Besides, it was awkward to have your parents drive you on a date.

During eighth grade at Queen Anne School, I became friends with a seventh-grade girl in one of my singing groups. When I left the next year for Tasker Junior High School, we became fervent pen pals. Toni's letters helped me get through that excruciating ninth-grade year. The next summer I went to her house several times to play with friends in her backyard pool or play board games with her and her mother. I promised Toni that as soon as I had my driver's license, we would go out on our first real date.

Our '66 Ford had sporty hubcaps and a jacked-up rear.

The day after my 16th birthday I took and passed both the written and driving parts of my driver's license exam. The following weekend, I drove the 20 minutes to Toni's house in the same Ford station wagon that I used during the test. Her mother required that our "date" happen during the daylight, so we planned to go to an afternoon movie.

Her Mother's Surprise

When I arrived, her mother said that it was good I had a station wagon because she wanted to pick up some long items at the hardware store. She rode in the back seat on the way to the theater and took the car from me when we arrived. Toni was furious. I was perplexed. Her mother picked us up when the movie ended. Afterwards Toni and I drifted apart.

2. Did you try out for any sports, plays, or musical groups in high school?

And did having 3,000 students in a school built for 2,400 feel crowded?

No to both. Bowie was so big that the performing arts and athletic teams were two totally separate groups that each demanded total commitment. The coaches had no reason to coordinate with the drama and music teachers, except for the marching band, which was tied to the football team. Also, although the school had a band, it didn't have an orchestra for violinists like me. Only at a tiny school, like my former Queen Anne, could you be an "in-school" Renaissance man.

During 10th grade, I was taking my seventh year of violin lessons. Mom was driving me every Thursday to the hour-long lessons with the demanding but wonderful Mrs. Wardall. The lessons were in the sumptuous addition to her Montpelier-Laurel Levitt rancher.

My audition for the Prince George's Youth Orchestra had earned me a place among its second violins. One of girls I carpooled with was the virtuoso leading first violinist, Adrienne Harris. Our carpool drivers, Chris and Sonya, were two older girls who played the bass.

Fortunately, in the long run, my medical condition kept me from trying out for school athletic teams; otherwise I might have played soccer, football, or tennis for Bowie. Instead, I concentrated on academics.

The so-called overcrowding was never a problem. It was the reason we had our open lunch hour. I loved open lunch because most club meetings could be held then. As for the many temporaries, my Psychology class was in one. I enjoyed being in a classroom with daylight coming in from both sides.

My brother Jeff was at Bowie in 10th grade during my senior year. He and a group of his friends had somehow painted the football field's two H-shaped goalposts and the many posts lining the track to look like candy canes before Christmas. From the windows of the breezeway, everyone marveled at the overnight prank. However, when Jeff and his friends next tried painting the roofs of the temporaries, they were caught by the police before they could paint any more than "Happy St. Pat."

3. Being close to Washington, DC, were you aware of national /international news?

During my senior year I joined our school's Political Affairs club. The club sponsor, Mr. Romeo, was surprised that we didn't know much about overseas events and suggested we subscribe to either *Time* or *Newsweek*. I started subscribing to *Newsweek* to augment what I was learning from my board game simulation magazines. The free museums and tours of the Capitol in nearby Washington, DC, had been taken for granted by most of us.

Mr. Romeo

Our club spent a weekend at the North America Invitational Model United Nations (NAIMUN) in a hotel in Washington, DC. Our role was a passive one because we represented the quiet countries of Bolivia and Switzerland. Among the thousands of high school kids, some play-acted as citizens of their country. The Palestinian delegation charged into a big council meeting with fake weapons and kidnapped an Israeli delegate.

4. Did you do other types of things with your friends during high school?

Many, such as:

A. Daytrip Skiing

Every winter in January and February, a bunch of us would pile in a car and go for a day of skiing at Roundtop or Liberty. John Cook remembers crowding four of us in his tiny Civic hatchback. These ski resorts were less than two hours away.  Before going, we would call an "independent" phone number for a cheerful recording that gave up-to-date slope conditions.

Unfortunately, ski traffic on the slopes on busy weekends quickly turned the powdered snow to hard ice. This was especially true on Martin Luther King Day, a not-yet-national holiday on a Monday in mid-January. Liberty's new back slopes would be powder covered until they were discovered by the masses. During a local "teacher in-service day," we enjoyed the luxury of sparsely populated slopes and lift lines. Our ignorance of Rocky Mountain skiing was bliss.

Often when the slopes had turned icy, we would trade in our long rental skis for short 135cm ones. These made it easier to ski backwards and do tricks. One trick we liked to do on the gently sloping straightaways was skiing through each other's legs. Four of us would ski in a column. The front skier would "snowplow" and spread his legs while the rear skiers would lay back on their skis and go through before standing back up. Then the new front skier would snowplow and so on. It was dangerous when someone went through and pointed their sharp poles at you. Many funny crashes happened before we perfected the trick.

B. Ushering for Diplomat Soccer

During the professional soccer season, Dad would drive a station wagon full of BSA soccer players to RFK stadium in DC. By volunteering to usher at Washington Diplomat games, we were given free tickets. We would each slip on an usher pinny and take our spots. Their bright yellow material around our bodies made us stand out. Although the home team, nicknamed the "Dips" (short for Diplomats), often lost, it was exciting to see pro tactics and strategies.

We helped people find their seats in our section. Die-hard fans knew their seats, but many people had trouble with the painted section numbers and row numbers. The seat numbers were on a tiny plaque on each seat.

One Sunday we were shocked that the stadium had been repainted, obliterating all section and row numbers. One of my first customers was a black man in strange clothes with a long line of people behind him. When I kindly said hello and asked to see his ticket, he obviously couldn't understand me. In a very strong accent he replied, "Section 2-4-5; Uganda embassy."

Thanks to my *Newsweek* magazine subscription, I knew about the brutal dictator of Uganda, Idi Amin Dada. He was a former heavyweight boxer who killed many of his own people and even boasted of eating children. The huge guy behind this nervous, dark-skinned translator looked very much like the dictator and gave me a very intimidating glare.

Before I knew it, these and other Ugandans filed past me. They included a couple of heavily veiled women, about seven children, and a couple of bodyguards. This odd but impressive foreign group went down and seated themselves in a random row.

Thanks to my having previously ushered in that section, I was able to seat many other fans in their correct rows. Then the Ugandan problem came to a boil. A group of irate men came up to me waving their tickets. I had to go down to the Ugandans and explain that they were in the wrong row. Thankfully, they acquiesced and moved back to an empty row. I hoped that their "translator" wasn't later shot.

Pelé

For the last game of the season, the usually pathetic RFK crowd more than tripled in size because it was to be the last league game for visiting Cosmos player Pelé, the Brazilian superstar. After this season, he was retiring from soccer. At the time he was probably the most famous athlete in the world. His prowess with the ball was magical to watch.

That day we also served as "end-game security." Near game's end, we stood around the field equally spaced and facing the crowd. Of course, we spent most of the time looking over our shoulders at the game.

When the final whistle blew, Pelé ecstatically ran off the field to our corner, ripped off his jersey, and threw it in the air. My brother Jeff and I were the closest to where Pelé's jersey landed. It was tempting to turn and run for it, but breaking ranks might have caused pandemonium. Soon players ran to it and tore off pieces to keep as treasured mementos.

5. What did you do to prepare for college?

There was a course requirement list for college entry, but it was nebulous and unconfirmed. Every college had very different and changing requirements. We were misled into thinking that most universities required four years of either French or Spanish. I chose French because it is the language of architecture (façade, fenestration, colonnade, etc.). However, it was trés difficile pour moi. If I had six hours of homework, three would be spent on French. However, later in life it proved more useful than I could imagine.

I had witnessed 12th-grade students at Queen Anne preparing for and applying to college. I learned you needed to have more than just a good grade point average. Acceptance into architecture school required going far beyond the minimum. That is one reason I worked so hard.

6. What was it like to apply for college?

There were about 17 universities that offered a professional architectural degree program at the time, and I preferred the ones that had a five-year intensive B. Arch program rather than a "4+2" program. The 4+2 six-year programs resulted in a professional M. Arch degree that was equivalent to a five-year B. Arch, but much more expensive.

Back then we didn't have fancy brochures and online comparisons of different colleges. As for a mentor, I hadn't even met an architect. From reading a few lines in a book in the guidance counselor's office, I narrowed it down to three East Coast five-year schools: UMCP, VPI, and UVA. Due to my fascination with MIT, I also applied there, even though it had a 4+2 program.

My parents went with me to UVA's beautiful campus to meet with its Architecture School admission officer. The most memorable thing he said was that they receive many very impressive applications but only accept one out of every six. Dad also brought me to visit Princeton, but the projects I saw in their studio didn't impress me. For instance, one guy explained his solution to the problem of "designing a restaurant to reflect Dante's *Inferno*." Its dining area spiraled down nine floors to the kitchen. Years later I'd know this as "Talk-itecture."

University of Maryland's architecture school had granted me early admission. Some of my scholarship money could only be used for an in-state school. During my visit there I parked the VW bug on Campus Drive near the Architecture School, but due to my excitement, I locked my keys in the car. Then it started raining very hard, so I climbed over the railing to get onto the covered back porch of a nearby dorm. Inside I found a payphone. While calling Dad, I discovered it was "Queen Anne" dorm, the name of my old school! Years later I would be living there.

MIT's acceptance was a two-step process. In my essay application I mentioned enjoying listening to speakers such as Edward Teller and Buckminster Fuller at lectures at my father's employer, NASA. Sometimes it doesn't hurt to "drop names." The application earned me an interview. An elderly alumnus called to set up an interview at the

Hot Shoppes restaurant in Silver Spring. After passing this, I was fully accepted. MIT held a monthly series of events for all the Washington-area acceptees: lectures, happy hour socials in Georgetown, etc., and I attended some of these.

The lecture that made the biggest impression on me was held in the Air & Space Museum's IMAX Theater. It focused on the pioneering stroboscopic work at MIT by Edgerton (who sounded to me like a historic polar explorer but was still living at the time). The images on the big screen included the now-famous extremely slow-motion movies of a drop landing in a glass of milk, a balloon being pierced by a bullet,

"The Golf Swing" by Harold Edgerton

and a golf club's swing. All were at an impossibly high resolution. The most memorable statement was that if we look in our Physics books we'll see his name on these and any similar images. It was true.

The daughter of the owner of Rodmans ("The Weirdest Little Drugstore in Washington" per a later article in the *Washington Post*) encouraged me to attend MIT with her. However, MIT cost $8,000/year, three times the cost at Maryland, and their best scholarship offer was $500/year. Discovering that MIT's Architecture undergrads were not considered good enough for their professional master's program made me realize it would all be for naught. Maybe I could go to MIT later.

Among the other three schools I had been accepted to, it seemed that UVA was currently only riding on its reputation, per my friend Doug after his visit. So, it came down to VPI and Maryland. Both had excellent architecture schools, but VPI was in the middle of the woods and I was interested in Urban Studies, so I chose the architecture school near the nation's capital, University of Maryland.

About the Author

Gordon Mead Stewart is an architect who grew up in Bowie, Maryland. His architectural work ranges from a timber-frame retreat on Virginia's Northern Neck to an office/retail/parking tower that includes a monorail station in downtown Seattle, and from a childcare building in West Virginia to a radar station in Honduras.

His Parisienne wife, Jacqueline, works as a scientist at nearby NASA Goddard. Her desire to raise their family in Bowie probably helped spark these memories. Since 1992 their home has been a Levitt colonial on Belair Drive facing Bowie's "tree tunnel," a bridle path lined with beech trees.

Like their father, the couple's son and daughter both attended Kenilworth Elementary. They played on soccer teams that Gordon coached over the years. He played indoor soccer on his architectural firm's team in the late 1990s.

When both children were in middle school at Holy Trinity, Gordon and Jacqueline created a school "Botball" team for them. The autonomous robots that the team of kids programmed and built out of Legos did well enough in the regional meet to qualify for the national meet in Seattle. There, against 89 other teams, they came in fourth.

In 2001 Gordon was awarded Bowie's Outstanding Citizen award. At the time, he was running BRAVA (Bowie Regional Arts Vision Association), a nonprofit that he founded and led from 1995 to 2004.

BRAVA coordinated between state, county, and city government, businesses, and citizens to plan, program, design, raise funds for, and build a state-of-the-art, 800-seat, balconied performance center attached to Bowie High School. Completed in 2004, the $14 million BCPA (Bowie Center for the Performing Arts) includes an orchestra pit, full fly tower, and 200-seat black box theater.

CPSIA information can be obtained
at www.ICGtesting.com
Printed in the USA
LVHW071137280420
654509LV00011B/973